Shadowed Oath

A Paranormal Romance

Stevie O.

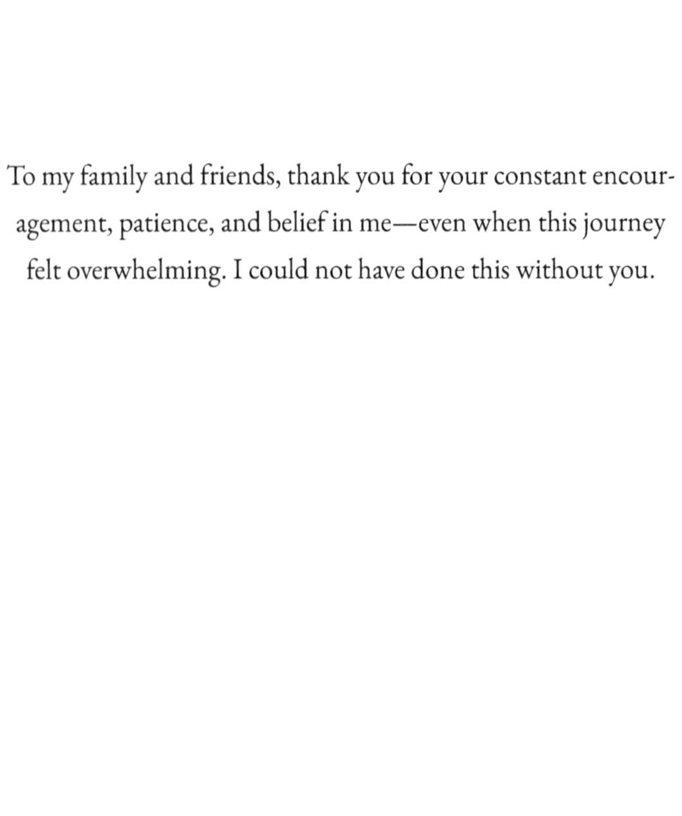

To my family and friends, thank you for your constant encouragement, patience, and belief in me—even when this journey felt overwhelming. I could not have done this without you.

Edited by Tori Moore with All That & Moore Services

1st edition 2026

Contents

Trigger Warnings

Content Advisory

This book contains themes and content that may be distressing to some readers, including:

-Supernatural violence and bloodshed
-Mentions of past trauma and emotional manipulation
-Intense fight scenes
-ptsd,
-murder,
-child sex trafficking,
-miscarriage
-Sexual tension and mature situations (18+)

While this story blends romance, action, and myth, your emotional safety matters. Please read with care.

— Stevie O.

A PARANORMAL ROMANCE

SHADOWED Oath

ONYX HUNTRESSES BOOK 2

STEVIE O

Prologue

Bayou Grisé, Louisiana. Home of wild hurricane seasons and scorching summers. Grisé Academy is out for the 2003 summer season, so outside was the only plans we had. Hurricane season was here, and our outside time was limited. We were out enjoying the weather while we could.

"Look at me, Lu! I learned a new trick." Jumping rope in the front yard was *the* pastime. The rope whipped loudly, cutting through the air as the rope moved faster. The successful criss-cross had my heart swelling. My two French braids flapped on my back as I picked up speed.

"Cool! You not better than me though."

My skin, flushed with a beet-red tint, glimmers with sweat. The tall oak trees were not enough to provide the shade we need.

"Lis, I'm going in to get a snack. Want one?"

Shaking my head no, I continued to jump rope and try new tricks. Suddenly, the air grew thicker, and the little breeze of relief we received from the wind stopped. The other kids in the front yards seemed to have stilled. Left! Right! No one else noticed the eeriness surrounding us. Silently, a white van with no windows moved slowly down my street.

No faces.

A figure covered from head to toe jumped from the back of the van. He ran toward me. My feet. They feel like they're stuck in deep mud. My voice. Gone. My brain. Stuck.

Swiftly, I was heading toward the van with a gloved hand over my mouth. A single tear fell from my eye as my brain realized I was being taken. Lu! Mamí! Papí! I reached for the house, with the hope that someone will come outside.

As my back hit the side of the van, darkness took over my sight, the smell of burned rubber and tires screeching took over my senses. A pinch to my neck made it all fade away. My family, my house...my life.

Chapter 1

Lucien "Shadow" Marceau

Now

Rain pattered softly on the front windshield of my White Mercedes, hypnotizing my mind with the mundane tempo of the rain sound. This allowed my brain to relax before the chaos of the day. The quiet hum of my S550 drowned out the thoughts that raced through my mind. Whispering to myself, "Today is going to be a good day. Bringing me closer to my goals." My daily affirmations helped get my mind right since this journey to Florida started in an effort to unearth the trafficking ring.

I felt everything slipping through my fingers, and I'm no closer to my goal of disrupting this organization. I was close to a big break in my discovery until I learned that the object of my last hunt was all smoke and mirrors. He was under the impression that medical supplies were being shipped in his transportation vehicles, but he was being used as a front for moving kidnapped children across state lines. He had no clue and was forthcoming on all the details he had available. Gruesome death was a great motivator for cooperation. As I thought about my latest failure, the tightness grew in my shoulders. Pulling out my chain from under my shirt, I rubbed the red bracelet I added to my platinum Cuban links chain as a constant reminder.

As the rain shower decreased, I took a deep breath and walked into my company as Lucien Marceau, successful CEO of Marceau Foundation—A non-profit for families and victims of trafficking. The organization helped them recover and excel after a life-altering situation plagued everything from their mental health to their financial situation.

"Good morning, Ms. Sharon! Any messages for me?" I walked into the building that had been nicely decorated by my assistant Sharon. She was like a second mom to me. She was the level-headed balance I needed in this organization, since I tended to take on more than I should when it came to this business. She was also very discreet in...alternative methods we turn to in times when they are needed.

“Good morning, Mr. Marceau! Yes, you did receive a message.” Reading from her notes, she said, “County Commissioner Daxton Levi is next up on your list.” She looked up at me over her glasses and gave me that Black mama stare. Her voice low and tone serious, “You be careful, Shadow. His file is on your desk.”

“Yes, ma’am. Please clear my calendar for after lunch. I won’t be returning to the office.”

Walking back to my office, I plopped down at my giant wooden desk. Looking around the huge space, guilt overwhelmed me. This big, beautiful building, office with a wall of floor-to-ceiling windows and a luxury vehicle plus a toy. All of this meant nothing when Lisette could still be out there waiting for me to save her. Her life ended, and mine was still carrying on like the best part of me wasn’t missing. The pounding in my temples caused me to sit back in my seat and close my eyes for a few minutes. Rubbing my head, I needed to accelerate this process before it killed me.

Lunchtime

Stepping out of the matte black pickup truck, I saw exactly who I came for. Perfect timing. County Commissioner Daxton Levi, the man of the hour. Dressed in all black, I walked along my truck, I quietly stalked up to the building from the almost deserted parking garage. I waited until he was done with his fake ass conversation before I decided to address him. “You should really pick your head up when you’re walking. You never know who is lurking in the shadows," I stated calmly with my gloved hands crossed in front of me.

His breath hitched as he looked into the dark space of the parking garage. "Wh-who is there?" Body shaking, voice trembling, betraying him, letting me know he was exactly who I thought he was. A bitch.

I moved out of the darkness and showed him my face. "Mister Commissioner, you don't know me, but I have reason to believe you are involved in sex trafficking children." As those words left my mouth, my mind was taken back to a more chaotic time.

"Lis, I'm going in to get a snack. Want one?" She shook her head no and continued to jump rope. Mamí was playing Summertime on the radio as I grabbed some fruit from the kitchen. Heading back to the front yard, I heard tires screech and smelled the stench of burnt rubber. The jump rope was abandoned, a red tennis shoe left behind. Lisette gone.

Daxton murmured something, but my brain didn't process it. Heat spread through my body, my vision blurred, and my mouth dried. Clenching my fist and gritting my teeth, I asked, "Who is running the operation? I know it's not you. You're too dumb." He had the nerve to look offended. I needed the info on who was at the top to dismantle the whole thing. If I could save families from going through what mine went through, that would do it for me.

I took another step closer to Daxton and could feel his pulse rapidly beating in his body. "I-I don't kn-know. I get paid to enact a certain policy. I don't have anything to do with trafficking."

"How does it work then?" By this time, I had grabbed him by the collar with one hand and was choking the life from him with the other. Voice low and menacing as I practically growled in his ear.

"I get a file emailed to me named the amount I am being paid. Inside, it has the policies I am responsible for and how I need to do them. There are no explanations as to why or who it's coming from. Once it's done, the money is deposited into my account." He was snotting and shit all on my black joggers. He doesn't get a pass like the transportation man. This situation was different. He knew something nefarious was going on and never bothered to check it out. Anyone could buy him.

I'd heard enough. "Kids deserve better," I said as I punched him in the nose. Blood sprayed from his face as his body collapsed to the ground. He lay in a fetal position, holding his face. Picking up my size thirteen steel-toed boots, I stomped his chest and face until I felt better. As I bent down to confirm that the life was drained from his body, I took out a scalpel from my hoodie. Just in case my boots didn't complete the job, this scalpel would finish it.

4hrs later

The rain had returned about an hour before the police showed up on the scene. My black truck had already been moved off the premises so that I wouldn't be questioned. I sat and watched as the cops pulled out the yellow tape and blocked off that area of the office building. Bystanders couldn't help their curious nature, even in the rain. Then a cobalt blue Audi S8 came flying into the area. Leading the way was a bushel of honey brown curls.

Ms. Keisha Grant.

I have wanted her since I first saw her in person. Her file was impressive, and Keisha in person was even better. Her aura preceded her. A natural vibe. She was a highly decorated detective, newly single with a good head on her shoulders. She actually cared about solving and preventing crimes. I wanted to get to know her in the worst way.

Keisha had crossed my mind every day since we ran into each other at Lucky's Wingspot.

Standing outside the restaurant talking, a little caramel cutie walked up and spoke to my acquaintances. She looked up at me and smiled with those mesmerizing eyes that had a slight hint of blue. Her lips were calling my name. She stared into my soul, and I returned her intensity. She didn't flinch and wasn't intimidated by a big man looking at her in that manner.

In another life, she would be mine. Her vibe matched mine and everything I would want in my woman, but I couldn't have that in this life. I needed to stay focused on finding Lisette's abductors.

Watching her move through that crime scene made me want her more. Maybe if I just hit it once, I could get her out of my system. I haven't wanted a woman like this since my ex, Dee, that's been a few years now. Yeah, I had women keep me company when I called, but I wasn't keeping them around much after that.

Starting my truck, I decided to head home to shower and rest my body for work tomorrow. Another day, another step closer.

Chapter 2

Keisha Grant

My alarm blared through my phone's speaker and jolted my body upright to alert me to get to the gym. Every morning at the same time, I was up and headed to the gym in my neighborhood. Being a panther shifter, my body stayed in pretty good shape, but I couldn't afford to let my human body slip. I've seen shifters who were caught slipping and were bested in a battle because they didn't stay on top of that workout regimen.

In my all-black high-waisted leggings, sports bra, and an oversized shirt, I headed to Ms. Sapphire. The name I had given my dream car. A cobalt blue Audi S8 with merlot interior. SZA played as I took the short trip to the gym. Even though the rain had been off and on all morning, I needed a good playlist to get me in the mood to burn these calories and get my heart pumping.

The gym was deserted, just the way I liked it. A steady drum of rain beat hard against the glass walls that covered three out of four walls and created a gloomy vibe. The cloudy sky, painted blue-ish gray, showed no chance of sunshine for the day. My panther craved to be set free to enjoy the rain and cool breeze. If I had time, after my gym session, I would let my panther roam for a few hours. In between sets of my bench press workout, my song was interrupted by Siri's voice. Ugh!! Rolling my eyes, I let out an exaggerated exhale and sighed.

Wilton Cartwright.

The ex that won't go away. We had been broken up for at least six months now, and he couldn't seem to take a hint. Hell, he called more now that we weren't together than he did when we were engaged. Pausing my music, I finally answered the call, sounding as dry as I possibly could, "Hello."

"Hey, baby. It's me, Wilton."

"What do you want, Wilton? I told you for the hundredth time that we aren't getting back together. I don't care how many therapy sessions you signed up for. You fumbled a good thing."

"I know, baby. My therapist made me see where I went wrong. In an effort to keep you, I pushed you away. You know I'm used to losing everyone I loved."

As he went on, I pursed my lips, crossed my arms, and waited until he was done with yet another sob story. He failed to mention to his therapist that he gaslit me every chance he got. I wanted us to work so bad that I would deal with his mood swings, his temper tantrums, and his name-calling. I would just try to work harder at not pissing him off. He even grabbed me around my neck a few times in anger.

Now normally, I would be down for a little rough play, but he wasn't in that mode. He had gotten in my mind and manipulated me so much that I forgot that I could snap his skinny ass in half with my bare hands. I was so in love that I forgot who the hell I was. I was one of the best damn detectives in Florida.

"I'm glad for your progress. Is that all?"

"I am going to work hard so we can be together again. I'll prove to you that I can be trusted with your heart, again."

Beep!

Saved by the bell. Another call beeped in my ear as he was doing his routine. "Wilton, somebody is calling. I think it's my job. I have to go."

"Ok, baby. I'll talk t-"

The call disconnected before he could finish, because I was over it. "Grant, we have a Homicide up here at the Bering business building. We need you up here. This one involves a politician. High profiles are your specialty."

"Ok. I'm in the gym, give me a few, and I'll be there." Packing my things, I abandoned my workout to head to the crime scene. I was on-call today, so I expected my phone to ring. An uptick in murders had plagued our little city as of late. There was no rhyme or reason to these crimes, so we weren't sure if this was a serial killer or just random killings taking over.

I took much longer getting ready than expected, so I had to push the speedometer a little more than usual. Putting the 500-horsepower engine to good use, I whipped into the area close to the roped-off crime scene. Even in the rain, people were nosey. The dark and dreary weather didn't deter bystanders, but, conveniently, I bet no one saw a thing. Stepping out of my car, I was met by a street cop eager to go over what they knew.

As he spoke to me, he eye-fucked me as if I weren't looking back at him. These men were all the same. Only good for hard dick and bubble gum. Sometimes the dick wasn't even that hard. I knew I looked good, but damn. I wore a tan suit with a black cami underneath. I finished the look with some simple black loafers in case I needed to get after a suspect tonight.

"We couldn't get a lot of info on what happened. The rain washed away a lot of the evidence we could have used. What we do know is this is County Commissioner, Daxton Levi." We walked fast through the rain as he debriefed me on the situation. There wasn't much left to say since my crime scene was destroyed by the weather.

I kneeled down to take a look under the white sheet. The victim's face was pummeled beyond recognition. The cherry on top was his throat was also slashed. The killer wanted to make sure he was good and dead, I guess. Standing straight, I looked over to our nosy crowd of people to see if anyone looked suspicious. Killers tended to stick around or came back to the scene of the crime. They want to see how their work was being received by the public and the department.

This was going nowhere, and my hair was getting soaked. I needed to interview a few bystanders, check any camera feeds, and check the victim's vehicle before the coroner made it out to grab the body. Every little bit I could gather would help me get closer to who did it and why. If I could get the crowd to disperse, I could let my panther out a little to rummage through the car. My panther's senses were more perceptive than my human ones. That was how I had been able to crack a lot of cases. You have to use what you got to get what you want.

After coming up blank with cameras, witnesses, and the car, I decided to head to the station to do some paperwork. This was a bust, but I'll keep searching. We don't want the residents of Blackwater to start worrying about their safety. My body was tired and needed a real break. This was my last day before a three-day off period.

Lying in my bed, I was thankful for an off day. Kinda. I was off from Blackwater PD, but I still had a few errands to run. I needed to be ready with my dish for the get-together at Nia and Xavier's house tonight. *I'll just stop by Lucky's Wingspot and get something,* I thought to myself. Anywhere I could cut corners to lie here a little longer was good with me. This week at work had been brutal. There was an uptick in homicides, and no connections yet. We either had a manic serial killer on the loose or people are losing it around Blackwater.

Being a highly decorated detective, I seemed to be the go-to for these weird cases as of late. The evidence was washed away from the rain, the cameras mysteriously were not working, or something else crazy happened to make it impossible to solve. I guess it was all working in my favor to get me closer to that Captain position. If I was the one to solve this group of cases, I couldn't be passed over for that promotion. With my Panther, these accomplishments kept stacking up.

The sun peeked through my royal blue blackout curtains on my bedroom window and warmed my caramel skin, energizing my spirit. Hopping out of bed, I rushed to open the windows fully. Today I wanted the fresh air inside the house too. Being a panther shifter, I never missed an opportunity to connect with nature. My modest home sat on an acre and backed up to the forest. I liked my privacy and needed to be able to let my panther out to stretch on those busy days when the PD had me occupied most of the time.

Hot water beaded and rolled off my back as I finished my shower. A feeling of renewal ran through my spirit. *Cuff It* by Beyoncè blared throughout my home as I moisturized my skin, sprayed my body with my favorite perfume, *Sangria+Saffron* by Michael Malul, and dressed in my yellow and white sundress. A lightness settled in my chest as I enjoyed my alone time in my own space.

Finally, I couldn't put it off anymore. I had to dress for the party and head out to get Lucky's famous spinach dip as my contribution. I took a deep breath in and exhaled loudly as I stood to throw on some cute jeans and a burnt orange off-the-shoulder top. Strapping my brown sandals up, I grabbed a matching crossbody, tucked my Glock in my back, and headed out the door. That yellow sundress would have been a great outfit for tonight's shindig, but I never felt right leaving my house in a dress. It always left me too vulnerable and exposed, and those were two things I didn't allow in my life.

The cobalt blue Audi S8 shone bright in the sun, but the dirt was brighter. Headed to the closest carwash, I opened my sunroof, then let the wind finger my wavy tresses as I flew through the city. This feeling of extreme happiness overwhelmed me. Being off duty today gave me a rush like none other. It might have been time for a vacation. I wish my ex, Wilton, and I were still on good terms. I might have to look into taking my sister,

Aaliyah, with me somewhere tropical. She was the only other person I would travel with.

Rushing across the street to beat the oncoming traffic, I hurried into Lucky's Wingspot to grab the spinach dip that my family loved. "Thank you!" I said shyly and blushed as I walked past the big chocolatey something holding open the door. His eye contact was intense when he said, "You're welcome, beautiful." I remember seeing him before, but didn't remember his name. He was here talking with Jamilah and Daddy one day. I couldn't get myself together then, and it looked like he was going to have the same effect on me today. He took a slight step forward, "I would love to get to know you. What's your name?"

Who the hell was this person running my body? When did I become shy? The words were caught in my throat as I extended my hand, "My name is Keisha."

"Well, Ms. Keisha, the first time I met you, I said I would get your number the next time we ran across each other. Would you let me take you out?" He dug in his pocket, then passed me his phone to input my number.

"Well, sir, I don't even know your name. I don't just go out with strangers. You could be a killer or something." I chuckled and noticed he just smiled. His hazel-colored eyes pinned me in place, and my heart rate sped up. My panther was intrigued.

"My name is Lucien. You are definitely safe with me, pretty lady. Now that I have your number, we can schedule something for tomorrow if you are available."

"I would like that. I'm headed to a family cookout, so let me get in here and grab my contribution." I tried to step away, but he stopped me with that sexy rumble.

"So, you can't cook, is what you're saying?" he said, throwing his head back in a hearty laugh.

"Ha ha! I'm a busy woman keeping the streets of Blackwater safe."

He tilted his head to the side as I spoke. "Impressive! Don't let me hold you up from the family dinner. I'll call you later tonight."

"I would like that, Mr. Lucien," I said as I walked into Lucky's and headed to the bar.

I finally pulled into my garage and sat quiet soaking in the peace that my home brought. The get-together was awesome. I spent time with my sisters, and Xavier proposed to Nia. They were so cute together and it lowkey made my heart ache. Wilton and I were on track to get married until Aaliyah helped me open my eyes. His betrayal, his manipulation, all had me never wanting to trust a man again.

As I grabbed my leftovers from the party, I got out of my car to walk into my peaceful palace. My phone buzzed in my pocket, and a wave of cold ran across my skin. Throwing the box of leftovers on the counter, I hurried to grab my phone. The caller ID said Lucien Marceau. *Mmmm, so that was his full name? Interesting.*

"Hello?"

"Hello! Is this Keisha?" His deep voice vibrated through my phone's speaker and sent a chill down my spine. He had the type of voice you felt when he spoke. He could say the alphabet, and it sounded sexy.

"Yes, sir! The one and only." My smile was so big, I knew he could hear it in my words.

"How was your day? Hope it's not too late."

"It's not. I'm just walking in from my family cookout. How was your day?"

"It was cool. Better now that I get to talk to you." My eyes rolled so hard. I could see this man must've been a player, but my smile never left my face. "So are you available tomorrow for me to take you on a date?"

I had no clue how to handle this. A man pursuing me? After Wilton, I wanted to just be single for a while to get myself together. I didn't have time to date another man who would try to use and abuse me because of what he thought I could do for him. Wilton and my father have proven that people are driven by their self-interest. There was no real loyalty. It was only as deep as what you could offer them. My focus was on building up my accomplishments. This man scared me though. He had me giggling like a schoolgirl and thinking about allowing him to pursue me.

"Work has had me busy, and I need to rest my body. Maybe another time."

He chuckled, then said, "You don't have to run from me. But it's cool, I'm patient, Ms. Grant. I'll let you get some rest then. We will talk tomorrow."

"Goodnight, Mr. Lucien." As I hung the phone up, all I could think about was his massive hands on my body. The way he looked at me earlier today, such intensity. There was a strong feeling in the pit of my stomach that he wasn't going to let me run from him long.

Chapter 3

Wilton

"You messed this up, and you need to make it right." The patriarch of my family yelled at me as he walked away. Slamming the door as he left promptly ended the conversation and let me know exactly where he stood on this situation. The silence in the room was deafening. The pressure was suffocating since I wasn't sure anything would work.

Pacing the floor, I was going to burn a hole in the expensive Persian rug on the floor. I swiped my hand over my face as I thought about how I could win Keisha back. My family hounded me about making things right with her. She was a great asset to our family, being one of the top detectives in Blackwater Bay. We could use her intel to warn us of things or give us our next move. Everyone fell in love with her when she first came around.

My uncle especially loved the connections she could bring to the table.

Keisha was a good girl, the type to walk in a room and turn heads. She saw the attention but never entertained it. She tried hard to keep me happy, and if her nosy ass sister wasn't in our business, she would still be with me. I pushed her too far, and now she was gone. Still single though, so there was still a chance. I liked her enough, but I wouldn't say I was in love with her. I only proposed to keep her around. Things weren't always bad with us. We had some good times, but my mind wasn't on her like that. My family needed her, but I had messed up and put my hands on her one weekend, so I had to do something. My inheritance was on the line, and I couldn't lose it. That was all I had since I didn't continue to pursue my dreams of being a ball player.

Every time she came around, it was a reminder of what I had to give up because of her. I was headed to the NBA, but my family thought it would benefit us more if I took over the family business and married Keisha as a safety net. I didn't want to take over the family business, kidnapping women and girls. I wanted to do my own thing, make my own name. My Uncle's thoughts were that *IF* I made it to the NBA, then there was still no guarantee that I would be making the big money like the stars. He pressured me to follow in his footsteps.

I didn't mean to hurt her, she just reminded me of what life could've been. So I had to make it look like I was working on myself to be better for us. Going to see a therapist wasn't all that bad either. My therapist was helping me get through the disappointment of not pursuing my dreams. Since there was no other way out of this situation, I had to make the best of it.

Getting Keisha back was the only option for me. This had to work, and I was willing to do anything to see to it. I would be ever-present until I wore her down. She would be with me one way or another, by force or by choice.

Chapter 4

Lucien

Night air drifted in to my open bedroom window as I lay in bed, half naked after my shower, trying to decide if I wanted to call Keisha tonight. I sat in the bed with only light from the basketball game on the TV. She already curved my ass the other night when I asked her on a date. I could tell she was interested but hesitant for some reason. Probably a busted ass ex got her in her feelings.

I knew once I got her on a date, I would see what was wrong with her, then I could get her out of my system. Some type of flaw that would be a dealbreaker, like a gold digger or an airhead. It would be cool, not like I was looking for something long-term. My mind was set on avenging Lisette. Keisha was just a distraction right now. I found myself thinking about her and all of that hair laid out on my chest as we lay on the couch. Or her riding in my truck with no worries on her mind and no work in sight. These ideas had invaded my thoughts at work, and I needed this distraction gone.

Maybe she was boring. No conversation. I shook my head as I gave in and reached over to my wooden nightstand to grab my phone off the charger. Dialing Keisha's number, I waited for her sultry tone to pick up and greet me. The last conversation we had, the sound of her on the phone was a pleasant surprise that soothed the beast inside. I got the more relaxed version that day instead of the business Keisha.

"Hello?!" She rushed out as if she were juggling a few things in her hand when she answered.

"Did I catch you at a bad time?" I let my voice drop a few octaves to entice her to accept my proposal tonight. I wanted some alone time with her, but I wasn't going to beg.

"Uh, no. Hold o-. Ok, I'm back. I was just walking into the house with all of my grocery bags when you called. I was determined to bring everything in with one trip." A chuckle left my mouth as she confessed her struggle.

"Well, if you let me take you on a date, that's one day you won't have to cook. We both know you can't cook anyway." A loud cackle came from her end of the line.

"I can cook, man. I was just being lazy that day. Anyway. I'm actually available tomorrow night if you want to meet up somewhere."

"Meet up? How about I come scoop you from your house? Since you are the Po-po, just run a background check on me, if you haven't already."

"That was already done. You seemed to have checked out ok." Her tone was playful, so I went in to solidify our plans.

"So that said, I'll pick you up at seven o'clock. Be ready!"

"But you don't know where I live." She rushed out.

"I checked you out, too. I can't have a crazy stalker lady on my hands," I said with a cocky tone, then chuckled as she giggled from my words.

"Good night, Mr. Lucien. See you tomorrow."

As I settled in bed, nervousness washed over me. I was only doing this to get her out of my head. After tomorrow night, I was sure I will be able to forget about her and continue on my mission for Lis. The game watched me as I drifted off to sleep.

"Lis, let's go outside to play. I don't want to be in the house anymore." We put on our outside shoes to go jump rope. Lis loved red and always wore her red shoes with her red bracelet, no matter what outfit she chose. Climbing the tree in the front yard, Lis drew in the dirt with a stick. She moved on to jump rope when I wanted a snack.

"Lis, I'm going in to get a snack. Want one? She shook her head no, and those two French braids bounced in the air as she continued to practice her criss-cross. Suddenly, Lis is crying and reaching for

me. Help me, Lu! Why aren't you helping me! Lu! Please! Help me!

My body shot up in bed, a cold sweat drenched my body. My chest violently rising and falling as I struggled to catch my breath. The nightmares were coming more frequently, and now they are twisting. Tightness in my chest formed as guilt washed over me. I knew I needed to stay focused on Lisette. She needed me, and I failed her. Rubbing the red bracelet I had attached to my chain, I needed to stay focused. "How could I have let this go on so long?"

I'll get focused after this date. After I get over this damn girl. I had to get her out of my mind so I could focus on what's important.

Debating whether to get up and take a shower now, my phone lit up with a missed call. My ex, Dee. Knowing she didn't want a damn thing, I locked my phone, rolled over, and fell back to sleep.

Monday

Work was long as hell and uneventful, but being back at home, getting ready for my date with the fine ass Keisha Grant, had me in a better mood. Dressed in all black, I chose a button-down with the top two buttons open for my platinum Cuban Links chain to show. I smelled like a million bucks, Naxos cologne by Xerjoff always turned heads. The sweet and warm spicy scent drove the ladies crazy. Tonight, we were riding in the white beast for a luxury vibe. The soft, leather peanut butter interior set the tone for a sexy night ahead.

Maxwell blasted throughout her home as I walked to her door to knock. The area was quiet, with the next house about a mile away. The forest that the house backed up to let me know she valued her peace.

Shit! This might have been a bad idea. The door opened, and a waft of a sweet, fruity smell nearly knocked me off my feet. The view and the smell of her had my senses in overload. She wore a burgundy silk halter top pantsuit with her back on display. What a beautiful, sexy back it was, too. She had some shimmer shit on it too. Her cleavage peeked out the top of the outfit, and I had to bite my bottom lip to keep from saying something crazy. Ms. Grant was killing it in that pantsuit. Her normally big hair was pulled up in a curly style and left all of her clavicle exposed just for me. This was a far cry from Ms. Detective lady who was all business. She topped the look off with modest gold jewelry and gold-strapped heels that showed her white pedicure.

"Hi, Ms. Grant. You look gorgeous!" She watched me with intense eye contact as I swiped my hand down my face. I needed to keep things in check, and she made it harder than I expected.

"Thank you! I'm ready if you are," she said shyly and extended her hand for me to help her downstairs. The sound of her door clicking ensured it was locked automatically as she closed it shut. We rode to STK Steakhouse with the low hum of R&B playing softly. I could tell she was nervous by the way she played with her purse straps in her lap.

We were greeted by the hostess and then escorted to our table. Placing my hand at the small of her back, I guided her through the restaurant as I watched our surroundings. You never knew who was around, and date or not, I watched my back. All eyes were on Keisha as we walked to our table. I made eye contact with every person mesmerized by my date to let them know what was up.

Her skin was so soft against my rough hands. Hands that have snuffed out life, brutally. I was on my gentleman shit with her. Keisha was so beautiful to me, she deserved nothing less. She sat and took in the ambiance of the modern steakhouse.

The back dining room was dark, only lit by wall sconces. This particular room provided a feeling of openness to the forest with a large window covering the entire wall. The mixologist sat in a corner bar to curate cocktails just for this room. Chandeliers and white tablecloths elevated the vibe to another level.

"This is a nice place. You did well, Mr. Lucien." She smiled softly as I sat back in my chair and sipped my water. Her eyes shone bright, with that unique hint of blue, like a kid in a theme park.

"It's cool. So, tell me, who is Keisha? Not the detective. Keisha outside of the PD." She looked surprised at my question. I sat back and waited for my answer. This is where I get my validation, so I could walk away. No more distraction.

Sipping her water, she thought about my question for a second. "I'm just a simple girl. I am a sister and a best friend. I love helping where I can and riding for my people that ride for me. I work a lot, yes, but I just want genuine love and fun experiences." She shrugged her shoulders like she didn't just say a mouthful.

The shrug was a downplay of her feelings as if they weren't often validated. I wanted her to know I saw her in ways that have nothing to do with that badge. As we stared into each other's eyes, the nervousness melted away a little, and she finally began to relax. "So, who is Lucien at your core?"

That question took me by surprise. She sat in anticipation of my answer, not just an inquiry posed because I asked her first. She wanted to know me. Not where I work, what I drive, or what I could do for her. Sitting back in my chair, I hung my head low and watched her before I answered.

"Lucien is a son, brother, a former military man, and a current businessman. I am just trying to tie up some loose ends for my sister and make her proud of the man I have become. Most of my time and energy is dedicated to that. Hence, the reason I started my foundation, the Marceau Foundation, in honor of Lisette Marceau."

As I told Keisha my story, I watched her emotions flash across her face. She held steady eye contact with me, but her features softened as I talked about the foundation. Talking about Lisette made my chest tighten again. I reached up and pulled out my chain and rubbed the red bracelet attached. I noticed Keisha's eyes watching my movements.

"This was the bracelet found after she was kidnapped. I had it added to my favorite chain. I never take it off."

"I'm sorry for your loss. That must have been hard. How old were you when it happened?"

"We were twelve. We're twins." Keisha reached out and placed her hand over mine. I glanced at her soft hands covering mine as they grounded me, kept me from spiraling in my thoughts about Lisette, like I normally do.

"I love how hard you go for your sister. It's been a long time, and you are still working relentlessly in her honor. I admire your resilience and perseverance."

Her words touched me in ways I wasn't expecting. This was not supposed to be happening. I sat up straighter in my seat and called for our waiter to get me a drink. Quick. Throughout the night, we talked more, and I couldn't even lie, Keisha Grant was pressure. She was fine, had a good head and heart. Triple threat. I wanted her more now than before, and I was afraid that if I got a taste, things might get messy. Obsessive.

As we finished our dinner, I decided I wasn't ready for the night to end. Quickly, I checked my phone for live music in the area. We headed out to hear some music and have a few drinks. Keisha let her guard down a little more as she danced in her seat to the vibe in the room. I was even able to get her up once to slow dance with me to So Fine by Mint Condition. As we swayed to the melodic sounds of the band, the feel of her body and the scent of her hair had me in a trance.

Shit!

With my hand at the curve of her back, I guided her to the car. Our night ended, and I couldn't have asked for a better first date.

The drive back to her home was quiet as we both rode the high from tonight's outing. Walking her to her front door, I wasn't going to push it, but I wanted to be inside her house, her mind, her body.

The Florida night sky, shone bright from the moonlight. The forest was the perfect backdrop to the modern elevation of her home. From what I saw at the front door, it was a modest home with a clean aesthetic. Keisha said her goodbyes at the door and then walked with a swing of her hips inside. This was all bad.

"Shit!"

Shaking my head, I strolled to my car with my thoughts preoccupied by a pretty lady who didn't know how dope she was. This was definitely going to be an issue. What I thought would be a one and done situation, had me wanting to see her again. Talk to her again. Touch her again.

My house felt empty when I walked in and thoughts of Keisha being here with me plagued my mind. Pulling out my phone to text her, I saw a missed call. Dee. I wasn't in the mood to entertain whatever she had going on tonight. I went straight to my messages app and pulled up Keisha's name.

Me: I enjoyed your company tonight. When can I see you again?

The little dots showed up at the bottom soon after she read my message.

Keisha: *The feeling is mutual. I'll check my calendar and let you know.*

Damn! I was really feeling Keisha, and I wasn't going to let her get away that easy. I knew she was feeling me with the way she was hugged up under me at the jazz club while we listened to live music. The booth they sat us in was the perfect set up. She leaned her body onto my chest and bobbed her head to the music. On the dance floor she couldn't keep her hands to herself.

As I drifted off to sleep, the house temperature set to freezing, my mind wandered. Back to my sister, back to Keisha, and back to my work. I needed to go harder. I needed to get closer. Keisha was right, it's been a long time, and I should be closer to some answers than I was now. As the TV watched me, the same dream played out beneath my eyelids.

"Look at me, Lu! I learned a new trick." Jumping rope in the front yard was our past time. The rope whipped loud cutting through the air as the rope moved faster. The successful criss-cross had Lis smiling big.

"Cool! You not better than me though. Lis, I'm going in to get a snack. Want one?" She shook her head no and those two French braids bounced in the air as she continued to practice her criss-cross. Suddenly, Lis is crying and reaching for me. Help me, Lu! Why aren't you helping me! Lu! Please! Help me!"

Heart racing, I shoot up in bed only to see a pitch-black room with nothing but moonlight peeking through the curtains. Quick, shallow breaths invaded my thoughts as I practiced what I learned in therapy. I couldn't let Lis down. This thing with Keisha, I couldn't let it go any further, I needed to stay focused.

Chapter 5

Keisha

Kicking off my shoes, I padded through my home barefoot. The cold tile against my skin was a vast contrast to what I felt inside. I walked straight to the shower to cool off these raging hormones coursing through me. That big, handsome man just took me on one of the best dates I have ever had. Lucien Marceau.

The way he commanded a room when he walked in it, his demanding presence, all of it shouted "Boss". This substantial chocolate man had me ready to climb him like a mountain at the end of the night.

His confident demeanor exhibited control and influence, but with me, he was gentle. For him to have had such rough experiences early in life, then in the military, he undoubtedly handled me with care. His large hand on the small of my back to remind me he was there. His closeness reassured me that he had me tonight. He didn't want Detective Grant, he wanted Keisha. The question was, was I ready to give him Keisha?

My mind raced as I washed my hair. Gone were the carefully curated curls, and returning were the big, wild, natural curls that I loved so much. Finished, I moisturized my body then climbed into bed with a heavy mind. I enjoyed myself tonight, but this man had the world at his fingers. That kind of man couldn't be serious with one woman.

Ding! The lights on my phone flashed as the screen lit up to notify me of a text that came through. I knew my sister couldn't wait to gossip about tonight. Looking at my phone, a blush grew across my cheeks. Lucien was asking to see me again. Hesitating, I blamed my busy schedule for why I put him on ice. I needed my sister, Aaliyah, to help me with this one. I couldn't say I didn't enjoy being curled up under his arm tonight, but all of that would have to wait.

A few days later, while walking into the office, I got the usual stares. Men licked their lips like they wanted to devour me whole. Being the only female in this precinct and in a male-dominated field, this was the usual behavior. That was why I worked my butt off to prove that I was not a piece of ass to be ogled. I didn't screw my way to the top. This was hard work and perseverance. I was the highest-ranking detective in Blackwater, so I let them see what success looked like as I walked past with my head held high.

A knock at my glass door stole my attention from looking through my notes on the Commissioner case. My Sergeant strolled in with a determined look on his face that spelled more trouble. "Grant, we have another homicide downtown. This one should be fun," he said sarcastically. "The killer left his motive at the scene of the crime. The street cops said this was some real vigilante stuff."

My eyebrows pinched at the sound of that news. The last thing Blackwater Bay needed was a street vigilante. This couldn't be the work of my daddy, either. Usually, he told me who was up next so I could get in front of it if necessary. Good old Timothy Grant, the balancer, might have some competition if we do have a vigilante on our hands.

My dad had a business, the Onyx Hunt, where all of his daughters carried the title of huntress. If necessary, he would call Aaliyah or me in to do some work, but his main Huntress was Nia. Recently, my youngest sister, Jamilah, had been promoted to lead huntress. He believed that the world needed balance; no one-sided agenda should dominate any particular sector of the world.

I understood the idea of it, but my heart resided right here with Blackwater PD. This was my lane, and I had accomplished many things, solving crimes and helping the residents of Blackwater and Miramar Isle, Florida. Gathering my things, I packed up to head to the scene of the crime. Rush hour was a terrible time for a crime scene in the middle of downtown. People were getting off work and running right into the mess of my crime scene. It made it hard to scope things out and partially shift to let my panther snoop for evidence.

"Grant! Grant!" Sergeant Thomas walked across the street toward me with a pale, badly dressed, blonde kid. "Grant, we got a newbie here. Welcome your new partner, Carter Vincent!" he said with a counterfeit smile.

"Partner?" Grabbing Sergeant Thomas by the arm, I pulled him away from Carter for a chat. "What do you mean, I have a partner? I work alone," I whisper-shouted at him. I have never had a partner. Not even when I was a street cop, and I liked it like that. Why would they give me one now?

"Yes, you have a partner." He turned his head to face the wiry-looking kid standing a few feet away from us. "My captain called in a favor." He walked me a few more steps away from my partner, "It's his nephew." He gave me the oddest look. "We need to take care of him. He is...special."

Groaning, I turned my head to look at Carter, then back at Sergeant Thomas. "You owe me." He turned beet red, nodded his head, then turned and strolled away. Taking in a deep breath, I squared my shoulders and walked toward my new partner.

The sun was shining bright, the weather was perfect, and the crowds were forming to watch us work. Walking past Carter, I said, "Let's go collect evidence. Don't touch ANYTHING!"

Lifting the yellow caution tape, I walked into the roped off section that held all of the noticeable evidence. The hair on my neck stood up straight, and my heart raced. Something was happening to put my panther on alert. She whined inside while I tried hard to keep my composure.

Carter struggled to keep up with my stride as he slightly jogged to catch up. He pulled out his notepad and began to write down what he saw. Glancing over my shoulder, his annoying glare made me uncomfortable. Then he started asking questions—like passive-aggressive reminders for me and probing into my methods of investigation. My panther was ready to tear his head off his shoulders as we continued to canvas the scene.

When we originally walked up to the scene, a street cop passed me a wallet in an evidence bag. Our victim was a 37-year-old male by the name of Gerald Alder. A family attorney who worked in the building where his body was found in front of. The covered body showed no blood around it, so we may be dealing with a poisoning or strangulation.

Looking closer at the body sprawled out on the concrete, I noticed there was a folder in a resealable bag beside the man. I reached into the pocket of my black pantsuit and pulled out two pairs of gloves. I offered a pair to Carter, just in case he wanted to touch something. The crowds that gathered along the yellow caution tape speculated loudly about what had happened. I saw a few interesting people I needed to question once I finished gathering other evidence. A smoky lavender scent assaulted my nose and left me with confusion as to what it could be tied to.

Reaching down to grab the bag, my panther came to the surface to inhale the atmosphere. With superior senses, she could sniff out any poisoning ingested in the body. A loud scent of bitter almond invaded my nostrils, and a wave of dizziness hit me. I knew we were dealing with arsenic but couldn't mention it to Carter as to not raise any suspicions.

Standing to my full height, I turned to Carter, "See if there were any surveillance cameras in the area that may have seen any confrontations."

When he walked away, I looked into the plastic bag with the documents in it to see what was being covered up. The manilla file had several sheets of information proving the lawyer was involved in the kidnapping of children he once serviced. If the child was in CPS custody and a parent reached out, he would orchestrate the abduction. This file outlined everything we needed. Tucking the information under my arm, determined to keep this info for myself. The vigilante wanted me to see it for a reason.

Spinning around to look at the building ledges, my eyes caught a familiar face in the crowd. Why was Lucien here? Maybe he had some business to take care of in the building. Those eyes held me captive like a prisoner in a cell.

Lucien winked at me while I stood captivated, lips parted, watching him. My nerves fired all at once as I took in the debonair man that I was kind of avoiding. He seemed to be everything I wanted in a man, but it might be too good to be true. I couldn't trust it. He might be another man with ulterior motives, out to see what he could get from me and how he could manipulate me in some way.

"Detective Grant!" Carter stood behind me and called my name repeatedly. He startled me out of my daydream. Turning to see him with his notepad, he stated, "The cameras were jammed and didn't show anything."

Ugh!! Turning on my heels, I traipsed toward the crowd to get witness statements. Lucien was gone by the time I started my interviews, but he was still heavy on my mind. I would love for him to be this great guy, but what if he wasn't? I didn't really have time to nurse another heartbreak.

As the crowd disbursed, we wrapped up the investigation. The body was picked up by the coroner, and they would have an official cause of death within two weeks. I explained everything to Carter, and by the time we were all done, it was time to head back to the station, then home for the day. Body tired and hair a mess, I drudged to my car and slumped in the driver's seat.

There were several notifications on my phone waiting for my attention. The one that caught my attention was from Lucien.

Lucien: I don't like your partner. He couldn't keep his eyes off you. You looked beautiful, by the way. Let me take you out tomorrow evening.

Rolling my eyes, I locked my phone and put it back in my pocket. The smile that crept on my face betrayed the emotions I wanted to feel. I needed to keep him on ice to guard my heart. I would hate to have to kill him because he was yet another man who tried to play with me.

Chapter 6

Lucien

Striding to my truck after snuffing out the lawyer made me smile. Gerald was hand-delivering the kids to predators, and I couldn't let that slide another minute. Not even for info on my sister. I stayed longer than I wanted just to see Keisha at the scene. She was the only detective worth anything in this town, so I knew they would put her on the case.

She walked in looking good as ever. Her black custom-fit pantsuit, showing off her curves, had me all eyes. I noticed I wasn't the only one either. Sending her a text to watch out for this new nerdy-looking dude hanging around her, I needed her to be on guard with him. He must be an intern or something. As long as he stayed in his lane with her, he would keep his life.

They were getting to the questioning portion of the investigation, so I had to head back to my office. I didn't want to answer any questions since I had left everything they needed. It was time to get my mind back to my number one mission. Lisette Marceau. I should have left the crime scene a lot sooner, but I just had to see Keisha.

Pulling my big truck up to my spot in the parking garage, my phone began to ring. My face dropped when I saw it wasn't Keisha calling me. My mom's name appeared on the infotainment screen in my truck. I took in a deep breath before I answered. She tended to read me like a book whenever we talked, and I wasn't ready for today's session. "Bonjou mama (Hello mama)", I greeted my mother in her native Creole French. I spoke a few languages, but my mom, she made sure I never forgot my native language.

"Bonjou, mo chéri" (Hi, my darling). Are you staying out of trouble?" she said lightly, and I just knew she was smiling big as she said it. She loved giving me a hard time. "I have been dreaming."

She said that, then the phone went silent. This was her set up. "About what, mama?"

Silence. Then there was a long exhale from her end. "There is a girl. I like her. She is good for you."

Swiping my hand over my hair, I stretched to keep from dealing with this conversation. "Ma, I don't have time. I have the foundation that has my foc-"

"Chéri, you deserve to be happy. You walk around with this guilt like your 12-year-old self could have done something besides get taken too."

Sitting back in my seat, I dropped my head back on the headrest.

"I don't know, Ma. You don't think I should be focused on helping kids and families of trafficking? You don't think I should still be looking for Lisette? She was my twin, Ma, and best friend. I can't just do nothing."

"You listen yere, boy. Your life don't stop because she isn't around. I know you love your sister, but you deserve happiness too. With a good woman, Ché."

She was really on my back today. Hitting me with some hard knowledge. My phone beeped, as I thought of what I could do to defend myself. Dee again. She had been hounding me for some reason. I'd get back with her later. I'm sure it's nothing to stop my call for.

"I hear you, Ma. I just don't want to let Lis down. I'm still having those dreams of her calling out to me for help."

"That's your guilt working on you. I have been having dreams too. Of this new woman. She needs you." She paused and waited for it to sink in to my brain. "She is the one for you, Lu, and you gon' have to be patient with her. She been hurt before, but that's not the end of her pain. Especially if you choose not to be around. She needs you, my baby. You need her, too. There was a snake."

As soon as she mentioned a snake, my body tensed, and my jaw tightened. Snakes are sent in a dream as a warning. "You listening now, huh? The snake was around her a lot, made her put her guard down, and then bit her. You know what that means, don't ya?" Shaking my head was all I could do with this new information.

My skin prickled at the thought of the dream and the implications. I couldn't let anything happen to her. I may have failed my sister, but I wouldn't let it happen to Keisha, too. I didn't know what kind of hold she had on me, but I wasn't willing to find out what would happen if I wasn't around.

"Lu?"

"Yeah, Ma. I'm still here. Just taking it all in."

"I know it's a lot, but there is more. Lis is still alive. Now that I am back with a coven, we have been working on scrying. I couldn't find where she was, but I could tell she was still alive."

Ma grew up in witchery but decided to stop practicing when she met my dad. She never taught us or ever even brought it up. When she and Daddy split, she decided to go back to her roots. She kept a protection spell on me while in my military career.

"Well, I'll let you think on that, but, Lu, you're doing a good job for your sister. She would be proud of the man you have become and the work you have put in. So stop being a martyr for Lis and live your life."

"Ok, Ma! I love you!" Pondering on the heavy conversation, I sat stuck in my truck for a few minutes longer.

Walking in through the back door of my office, I wanted to bypass all of the workers since Shadow's work was done, and it was time for Lucien to clock in. Ms. Sharon received a notification that I was in the building and came in to greet me.

"Good morning, Mr. Marceau! We have an urgent matter on the books today."

She handed me a thick manila folder. As I began to look through the file, I gave her the side eye. I had no clue what she was talking about. We didn't have anyone else scheduled for this week. As my eyes read through the words, my muscles stiffened, and heat coursed through my body. A middle school teacher is using his position to pick out students with little to no parent involvement. Runaways or neglected students were taken more from that school than from any other district in the state.

My plan was to put an end to it today. I sat in my chair and looked out into the trees to ponder how people had become so corrupt. These were children who trusted the same people who preyed on their innocence. I needed to throw a wrench in future plans, at least.

The campus was a desolate building, which was odd for a weekday. There were no after-school activities? My next victim seemed to be the only one in the building. As I stood off to the side behind a column in a dark corner, I waited until the perfect time to strike.

The sun was descending from the sky, painting a beautiful pinkish purple canvas for tonight's events. What a lovely day to blow off some steam. My mind had been overtaken with thoughts of Keisha and the dream my mom explained. Quickly, as I advanced on my target, joy spread in my chest. I needed some activity today since I missed the gym, so I jumped in the air and came down on his neck.

His body fell to the ground, but I jumped back to give him time to recover. Ugh! He folded up in a ball and didn't even try to fight. What kind of shit was that? Bending over, I yanked him up by his collar. He was going to help me with this workout whether he liked it or not. Getting into a fighting stance, I threw a few jabs to his chin. He must have been made of glass because he kept folding. I was getting tired of picking his weak ass back up.

Finally, I broke a sweat and could conclude my little workout session. A right hook spun his body, an upper cut sent him back, and I caught him around the neck and squeezed until I was satisfied. I pulled out the manila folder, placed it in a resealable plastic bag, from my back and threw it on top of the trash. Couldn't have my baby working too hard to find the evidence.

Walking back to my truck, I took my leather gloves off and pulled out my phone. In the messages app, I scrolled to Keisha's picture that I grabbed from the file I had of her from the time I was investigating her family. I needed to see her big hair and natural face. Her authentic self was what I enjoyed seeing the most.

Me: Are you going to continue to hide from me, or are you going to let me take you out again?

Keisha: I am not hiding from you. I have just been busy. You saw me at one of my crime scenes.

Pulling out of the parking lot, I waited until I made it a mile away from the property to unjam the cameras. The evening weather was cooler than it had been all day. Lowering my windows, opening my sunroof, I sat back and rode home. Obviously, I was going to have to pop up on Keisha in order for her to see the seriousness of the situation. After talking to Ma, I planned to be all gas, no brakes for Keisha. I couldn't have her out here lacking the thing only I could give.

The moon shone bright on my residence, acting as the only light in the area. Moving in the shadows had become my thing since my time in the military. Most people needed light, but

I thrived in the darkness. When I moved up to a special unit, Intelligence Support Activity (ISA), our missions included a lot of surveillance in the darkness. We were a covert operation with no sanction to work in the U.S., so we had to stay hidden. That was when I received the nickname, Shadow. Being one of ISA's top operatives, I was known for quietly invading territories, eliminating targets, and extracting intelligence. All before they noticed there was even a breach in their security.

The world was shut out as the garage door slid closed behind my truck. I sat there in the closed garage to allow my eyes to adjust to the dark. Trudging past the kitchen, I dropped my things on the dining table and headed to the shower. After the day had been washed off and I was more relaxed, I lay in the bed, turned on basketball highlights, and FaceTimed Keisha.

Her beautiful face appeared on the screen shortly after the second ring. With tired eyes, she smiled, and I knew I was wearing her down. She loved our talks on the phone, the frequent texts to check on her, and she really enjoyed our date. When I get her to trust that I wasn't the previous dude, we would be ok. I needed this sped up because I took my Ma's dreams seriously. Something is in the works, and somebody is plotting against her.

After an hour of talking about her day, her new case, and how we may have a serial killer in Blackwater, we ended our conversation. She was opening up more, and our time was coming. I only had patience during a mission, but Keisha was going to make me work for this next date. Once I had her in my grasp, I wasn't letting up on her. She would be mine.

Chapter 7

Keisha

This man was persistent, he texted me often just to check in on me, even when I declined his date requests. He was patient with me and listened to me vent about this mysterious killer on the loose. This has been running rampant in my thoughts for a while now

I was grateful to have a day off to spend with my sisters. We had finally come together to schedule a day to go out for lunch. I love them, and we didn't spend nearly as much time together. After all of the drama with Jamilah came out, we decided to be more conscientious about enjoying each other.

Yes, we have our family dinners and the family panther run, but it wasn't until recently that Jamilah was even included in the run. Finding out she felt like the black sheep because she couldn't shift broke my heart. Now that her panther has surfaced, we make sure to invite her first. Jamilah was my baby doll as a little girl, and I made it a point to watch out for her. My heart ached for her when we found out our mother had an affair with our dad's best friend and got pregnant. Jamilah would always be my baby doll, no matter who her dad was.

Before getting ready for our sister lunch date, I decided to take my panther out for a run. The pent-up energy contained in my panther kept me on edge this last week. She wanted Lucien for us, but I was still unsure. Although she never really cared for Wilton. I just didn't want to repeat my mistake with jumping into something with Lucien, and he wasn't as solid as I thought he was.

There weren't any red flags that I could see yet. Maybe a little jealousy, since he was always asking questions about my partner. He seemed to think Carter was no good and that I should watch my back. Although annoying at times, I didn't get a vibe that I needed to watch my back from him. I have caught him staring at me, but who wouldn't?

As we ran through the lush greenery in the forest, the rhythmic thud of my paws slamming against the ground calmed me. The earthy scent of the woods mixed with the scent of flowers brought joy to my spirit.

Feeling lighter, I sauntered back to the house to prepare for the absolute foolishness to come with hanging with my sisters. The sun shone brightly on my golden skin. The run lifted some heaviness in my chest.

Lucky's Wingspot came into view as I turned on the street and parked. Looked like the gang was already here waiting on me. I plopped down next to Aaliyah as we ordered our drinks. She was such a sweetheart who had been through too much with men, but she was still optimistic about finding the right one.

Nia complained about our daddy calling her for more jobs. He obviously thought that since Jamilah was able to take over the lead huntress position, that meant he could increase the amount of jobs he took. Xavier was not having it though. I loved the way my new brother-in-law covered Nia when it came to her pleasing our parents. He would run interference any time he felt like she was falling back into the pleaser role with them.

Sitting there listening to them go on about daddy, Jamilah starts with her dramatics. She is definitely the more theatrical sister out of the bunch. "Baby, y'all are better than me," she said with that southern drawl. Shaking her head, she turned her attention to me, "Be glad that police department keeps you busy, or he would be on your line begging as well."

"Don't talk about my daddy. He is perfect," Aaliyah said, pouting, giving Jamilah a mean look.

"You are just saying that because he doesn't really call you about the Onyx Hunt. He knows you would want to have a talk therapy session with the person you are supposed to kill."

We all cackled at Jamilah clowning Aaliyah, but no lies were told. Out of all of us, Aaliyah was the most peaceful one. She had a good heart.

"He bothers me for inside info instead." I really felt a way about that, too. My daddy loved his girls, but he was always asking me to look into something or give him details about something. Just like how I felt about Wilton. He wanted something from me, and without it, I wasn't as useful to him. No real calls to check on me or take me out to dinner like he does with Aaliyah and Jamilah. Aaliyah says it was because he doesn't want to bother me due to my busy schedule. Once a month, just us would be good, but it was what it was.

"Both of y'all need a man so daddy can't try it with y'all," Jamilah said, then all eyes were on me. They all knew about a guy trying to take me out, but my schedule kept me busy. They knew nothing of Lucien, and I think I wanted to keep it that way.

Aaliyah was the sister I spoke to the most, so she had more of an idea of what I was dealing with. "You really should stop playing and give that guy a chance. You don't have a real reason not to."

Three pairs of eyes watched as I struggled to keep my emotions under wraps. A big grin spread across my face as my cheeks blushed.

Nia chimed in, "By the look on your face, he must be something. Who is it, sis? Tell us more."

"It's nothing, guys. We went on one date. We are not planning a wedding." Laughing it off, I hoped they would move to the next topic. I really didn't want to talk about Lucien with them.

"I don't understand what the problem is, sis. This man seems to be about something. Has his own business, all his teeth, and no red flags have come up in the daily conversations you guys have." Aaliyah just had to put my business out there. She knew I was scared to trust another man after Wilton. We were supposed to be planning a wedding, but instead, I was planning on how to duck and dodge his calls.

"Some of us would love to have a man who was genuinely interested. Calling you to schedule dates, not just texting, 'What you doing?' all day. Consider that a blessing. You know there is piss in the dating pool," Aaliyah continued on with her rant. I really felt for her. Her forgiving nature had caused more than enough heartache. It was past time for her to stop dealing with men who would mistreat her and lie. She wasn't really the pop-off type unless we were getting active in the field. Timothy

Grant didn't play that. He made sure you rose to the occasion when it came to training and working with the Onyx.

I knew me pushing Lucien away might feel like a slap in the face to Aaliyah. She knew I really liked Lucien, and I shouldn't let the man before him ruin possible happiness. "You right, sis, I'll do better. Next time we talk, I'll accept his invitation. I really can't tomorrow, though, I am scheduled to go out to dinner with the work crew. Maybe this weekend."

We continued on like that for another two hours, then walked out to our cars. Aaliyah and I stood at our cars and spoke some more about my situation. Just as I moved to get in my car, an overwhelming scent hit me. That same smoky lavender. Confused by what that could be, I looked around to see if there was someone watching me.

Unease settled in my shoulders as I pulled from Lucky's parking lot. The short drive home was uneventful until a call came through. Wilton. Rolling my eyes, I decided to ignore his same song and dance. He realized a little too late that I was worth more than what he was giving me. If I got back to that, it will be telling him I'll forgive anything, and I have learned to value myself a little more in these last six months. It was hard, but I was no longer accepting things I couldn't change. I was removing myself from things that no longer served me and my best interests. That also meant I was moving forward and allowing Lucien to show me what he had to offer. Scared and all. I didn't get to being the best detective in the city by moving scared.

The stale, stench of coffee circulated throughout the building. The overcast outside created a gloomy atmosphere in the station. I was dragging today with my mind anxiety-riddled on how to approach this new string of murders. My hair was pulled back in a ponytail, and I just threw on a royal blue pantsuit with a black camisole underneath. Not hearing Lucien's voice last night affected me more than I thought it would. His deep timbre is calming. Him only sending me a text didn't quite sit well in my spirit. Even though the text was a sweet thinking of you message, I would rather hear his voice.

Sitting in my office, I turned on a little music so I could concentrate on these files. I knew it wasn't a coincidence that these latest murders, all of the victims were a part of a nefarious scheme of trafficking children. Our killer has been leaving more than just bread crumbs as to why they were doing it, but we had to stop the street vigilante. The Blackwater residents were starting to feel uneasy.

Personally, I wasn't too upset about it since they were taking out the trash and keeping the kids safe. Unfortunately, I still had to get to the bottom of this.

What I knew was that the cameras tend to jam around the time of the murders. We didn't have any video surveillance from the direct businesses or neighbors in the area until close to the time when the bodies were found.

I did notice a black truck with the license plate blacked out about three miles down the road, close to the time of all three murders. I needed to see about identifying that vehicle so I could pull the registration. As I moved on to the next file to comb through those details, my phone lit up with a text from Lucien.

Lucien: I know you've been hard at work, let me take some stress off your plate and take you to dinner tonight.

Smiling at my phone, I suddenly realized I couldn't. Not because I didn't want to, but the work dinner was tonight.

Me: Can't tonight. I have a work thing to attend.

This wasn't just me avoiding him, I really did have this on my schedule a while ago. This was my department's effort for us to bond and bounce ideas off of each other. I couldn't bail on them.

Deciding to double text, I didn't want to leave him hanging. He has been asking me out for a while now. We have been having great conversations nightly, and I didn't want him to give up on me.

Me: Raincheck?

He didn't respond, but he could just be busy. I hoped. I knew I couldn't keep putting him off. I really did like him. Time to put my big girl panties on. As I finished the day up, I was ready to go home and get into bed, but had to pack up for the restaurant. Sitting in another Steakhouse, I marveled at the decor. Morton's Steakhouse was what the Captain chose, and since I wasn't paying, I had no complaints.

The guys ordered beer while I sat in a booth with a Washington Apple. I wasn't in the best mood to socialize since Lucien never responded to my text. My panther's anxiety rose a little more as I sat and watched the people interact. The booth was close enough to the bar to be included, but still tucked away so that I wasn't highly visible to the rest of the restaurant. That worked in my favor since the man plaguing my thoughts all evening walked in, but not alone.

Leaning back in the booth, I raised my glass to take a sip and watched over it as he and his date walked to the table. He looked good as usual with black slacks and a fitted black polo shirt. The muscles peeked from his shirt sleeves, and his favorite chain stood out against his dark skin. The hint of red was not to be missed and was a great contrast.

He didn't seem to be interested in the lady on his arm. She was all over him, but the vibe wasn't there. He was a gentleman but seemed preoccupied with something on his mind. As I watched, my jealousy heightened, and my panther was angered at me. She wanted me to stop denying him and us a chance to be something real. Guess I was right, he was a ladies' man, or maybe I pushed him to this with not accepting his offers on more dates.

I cut out a little early in order to avoid running into him and his date. My day was shot and seeing him on a date made it worse. I headed home to put on my pajamas, lay in bed and, drink some wine.

Chapter 8

Lucien

Keisha: Raincheck?

Looking at my phone, I blew out a long breath before I dropped it back in my desk drawer. I didn't even feel like responding right now. Rubbing my hand down my face, I needed to set aside some time to pull up on her. I said I would, but she couldn't keep running from me.

When we talked at night or texted on the phone, she was responsive and enjoyed our conversations. Ruminating over my feelings about Keisha and her avoiding me, I struggled to get any work done. In the wake of my procrastination, my phone rang and knowing it wasn't Keisha I was going to ignore it. As it rang for the third time, I grabbed it out of the drawer to find Dee calling.

"Hey, Dee! To what do I owe the pleasure of receiving, yet another call from you?"

"Hey, baby! You haven't been answering when I call, and I know you miss me. I miss you!" she said in a sultry, almost whiny tone. She was going to lay it on thick since I had ignored her calls.

"I been busy, what's up. You need anything?"

"Just you. I miss you. In my bed. Us being together. Going on trips."

And there it was. She missed me spending money on her and giving her attention. She must be going through a dry spell with men. Ran out of sugar daddies, I guess. We had broken up over a year ago because we wanted different things. She wanted more money. I wanted somebody who actually cared about me and not just my pockets.

"Why you so quiet? Let's go to dinner tonight. Come pick me up like old times and go out."

"I'm quiet because I'm working, Dee." Annoyed at her blatant disregard for my time, my tone was curt, hoping she would get the idea that I wasn't in the mood. Leaning back in my chair, I let it recline as I thought about my options. She would just keep calling and begging, might as well take her up on the offer. Besides, it wasn't like Keisha was giving me any play right now.

I wasn't giving up on her, especially if what Ma says was truth. Her dreams have never failed me, so I was holding on to that. Maybe I could go out with Dee and relieve myself of some tension.

"OK, Dee. I will pick you up for 7pm. Don't have me waiting all night either. For real. I'll leave you."

I quickly ended the call so I could focus on my work. Guilt seemed to creep into my mind as the day went on. Confusion settled over me as I tried to make sense of this feeling. It wasn't like I was her man, yet. Couldn't do anything wrong when we aren't even together.

Keisha had been actively avoiding being with me in person, but she had to be scared of what we could be. Our first date was like none other. We fit together like we had been doing this for years. Talking on the phone like kids in school, but seeing her face-to-face was another story.

As the sun went down, I readied myself for the date, but I wasn't going all out for Dee. Simple black slacks and a black Polo would suffice. She was probably going to be dressed like this was more than what it was.

This was not two exes celebrating a reconnection. I'd never forget the things she said to me about my PTSD. She tried to handle me like I was broken, and that wasn't the case at all. I wondered what piqued her curiosity to reach back out this time.

Since I was a gentleman, I walked to the front door instead of blowing my horn. Standing at the door, an exaggerated sigh left my mouth. I was rethinking my decision now. Did I want to deal with Dee's shallow ass just to blow off some steam? This was heavy on my mind as I stood and waited for her to answer. I almost left.

The door pulled open, and she looked damn good. Her small frame was draped in a flowing Chiffon dress with her cleavage pushed to her chin. Her entire back was out until right above her ass crack. I could already tell what type of time she was on. She was mischievous, and that was how she always got me.

We rode in the beast to the steakhouse and were seated shortly after walking in. There was a prickly feeling under my skin as if I were being watched. Years of military training taught me to trust these feelings. Immediately, my back stiffened, and my eyes roamed the dining area to see if I recognized anyone. Nothing.

Throughout the night, the feeling intensified as Dee trampled on my nerves. Ready to get away from her touchy ass, I quickly requested the check. I had to use more patience with Dee than I did in a 3-day stakeout in the military. Every few minutes, she rubbed my arm and grabbed the back of my head. That used to always get me going, but this time it was a turn off.

As we walked out of the dining area back to the car, I made sure to scan the room for familiar faces. Even though the feeling was gone, I needed to be extra cautious. No one looked familiar, nor did anyone look shady.

The cabin inside the beast was quieter than a church mouse. Dee noticed the usual effect wasn't there. Things just would never be the same between us. Not even ass could fix the things she said to me. According to her, she was worried for her safety because my crazy dreams made her feel I would murder her in her sleep. She was embarrassed to have a man who couldn't "get over" the trauma I endured in the military. Oh, and my favorite one, my sister was taken over twenty years ago. It was time to move on.

"Lucien, I know I said some messed-up things in the past to you, but come inside so I can show you I deserve forgiveness. I want us to be the way we used to be."

"Dee, I'm not even on that anymore. I forgave you a long time ago, that doesn't mean I forgot." Putting the car in park, I got out and walked to her side to open the door. My thoughts were running rampant. I could be in and out in twenty minutes, feeling lighter.

She looped her arm in mine as we walked to the door. Just twenty minutes. Dee looked up into my eyes and smiled. She knew she had won this battle.

Getting inside, her home looked the same as usual. Cozy, well-kept, and an overall homey feel. Her bedroom was already set up for a night with a guest. She just knew her feminine wilds would win. She stepped into her bedroom after me and removed her dress. Her perky breast called out to me just as a wave of nausea filled me.

That feeling of guilt was back. Shit! I dragged my hand down the back of my head and rested it on my neck. The deep exhale had her pausing her progressing steps toward me.

"What's wrong? You don't want this?" she asked as she waved her hands down her tight bronze skin. She was a work of art. All of her sugar daddies paid hefty prices for this masterpiece.

This was a mistake from the beginning. I let her talk me into a whole date when I really only wanted one thing from her. Now that it was here, laid on a platter for me, I didn't even want it.

"Actually, naw. I'm good. Enjoy your night." I walked around her naked body straight out the front door. Blowing out a breath, I sat in my car thinking about the release I just walked away from. Keisha is the only one on my mind, and I never should have entertained Dee. I was going to pop up on her for sure this week.

Getting to the house, it was pitch black and quiet. Just the way I like it. I showered and lay in the bed for my nightly call to Keisha, but there was no answer. Probably sleep already.

This week wasn't nearly as hectic as last week, with all of those last-minute cases I needed to take care of. I actually had time to sift through files for the Marceau Foundation. The sun was shining bright into my office, giving me the energy I needed. The morning workout was brutal, but I had to get in some extra cardio to blow off some extra steam since I couldn't empty my balls last night.

Thinking about lunch had me reaching to call Keisha. This time I wasn't asking. As the phone rang, I sat back in my office chair staring out into the forest. Picking up on the third ring, there was a lot of noise in the background. She must have been out to lunch.

"Hey, baby girl! I'm coming to get you Friday at 7 p.m. so we can go on another date." I dropped my voice an octave so she would feel it instead of just hearing it.

"That doesn't sound like a good idea." The line went quiet. There were no excuses given. No alternative. Just a decline. Her voice was flat and detached. "Your girlfriend might find issue with that."

"What girlfriend? I don't ha-" In the midst of my response, I knew what she was talking about. She must have seen Dee and me last night. Shit!

"Ah, you remember now. I was in the restaurant with my co-workers. Guess you couldn't wait and had to find something warm to slide into. Typical." Damn, she was on my ass. Last night wasn't even worth it. I sat back in my office chair, putting my hand over my eyes. I tried to think of something to dig myself out of this hole.

"Keisha, I have been trying to take you out again since date number one. You have declined every invitation. That girl was an ex who asked to see me. Nothing more. Crazy thing is, I only thought about you during dinner. It wasn't even a date."

I heard someone in the background talking to her, but I couldn't make out everything. A feminine voice that sounded like it was on my side. Keisha kissed her teeth at whatever was being said.

"My sister, Aaliyah, is here with me at lunch. Apparently, she thought you had a point. Tomorrow at 7 p.m. is good with me."

As we ended the call, my heart rate slowed down. She wasn't getting away this time. It was time for Keisha to stop playing with me. She was making it really unsafe for Blackwater. Shadow came out to play, and not having what I needed made him a very scary man.

I was able to find some last-minute tickets to an All Black R&B experience for the date. We enjoyed the live music on the last date, so this should be right up her alley. Pulling into Keisha's driveway, this time I chose to pull out the truck. The matte black Ford F-150 with obsidian black tint was reminiscent of my alter personality, Shadow.

Keisha stepped out in a fitted black blazer with a tight top, black cargo pants, and black heels. The blazer sleeves were pulled back, showing the platinum diamond tennis bracelet, stud earrings, and a simple silver solitaire necklace. She cornered the market on simple elegance. Helping her up into the lifted truck, I grabbed her by the hips and gave her a push.

This date was more intimate. Since we talked or texted every night, she was more relaxed with me. I reached out to grab her hand and intertwined our fingers with no objections. I was done with her running. She was mine.

Chapter 9

Keisha

Riding in this massive, all-black everything truck had me feeling sexy. Walking out into the night air, the moon shined bright on Lucien's umber colored skin with red undertones. He glowed in the moonlight, and his muscular, tattooed arms called to my soul. I was taking my sisters' advice, letting things flow with us. I liked him and wanted to see where this goes, but I couldn't sabotage it before it got started.

As we moved across the city in this powerful machine, Lucien grabbed my hand and intertwined our fingers. His massive frame made my 5'6" body feel small and dainty. Especially when he grabbed me up by the waist to help me in the truck. Wilton could never. He was taller and lanky where Lucien was tall and muscular.

Being able to not take the lead was a relief. This was foreign territory, being taken care of was nice, and was not often received. We listened to old school R&B as we made our way to the venue. Stokely's voice, from Mint Condition, set the mood, and just like the first date, I was all up under Lucien before I realized it.

We sang, danced, and just vibed to good music. After the music, we found ourselves in an all-day breakfast cafe to soak up the liquor consumed. My panther was in complete awe of Lucien. I might be in trouble. She might not let me walk away after tonight.

Leaving the diner, Lucien seemed lighter and more relaxed but I noticed his head was still on swivel. From our long conversations on the phone and now spending time together, I realized my heart might be in trouble. One question lingered in the back of my mind: how will he feel when he finds out about my panther?

She was a part of me. We are a packaged deal, and unfortunately, she is already attached. She came to the surface and clawed at me to meet him. We had to wait a while longer since I hadn't even kissed this man. The mood was perfect, and we decided to head to his home.

We pulled up to a modest home that was pitch black on the outside and inside. The garage door pulled up, and he was able to fit that massive truck inside. Before we stepped out of the truck, Lucien leaned over to my side and grabbed my neck, pulling me to him. He rested his supple lips on mine, kissing me senseless. As I sat back to catch my breath, I giggled like a schoolgirl.

Inside the dark home, he led me to his bedroom without turning on a light. Normally, that would be weird for a human, but I had no issues because my panther had enhanced vision. Inside his room was a neatly made king-sized bed. His decor was typical for a single man, no frills or extra pillows.

"Are we doing this, or do you want to chill? I don't want to push you into something. I'm on your schedule."

I opened my mouth but couldn't find the words, so I shook my head yes. Lucien bent down and grabbed the back of my thighs to wrap my legs around his waist. He kissed me with all of the passion he could muster. As if he were trying to relay his feelings in a kiss. He sucked on my bottom lip, then licked them requesting permission to enter. As our tongues tangoed, my body melted into him like glue.

This man was pulling things out of me that I had never experienced, and I wanted more. He walked us over to the bed and lowered my body onto it. Grabbing my feet, he pulled my heels off, then sucked my toe in his mouth. The eye contact he held with me was like seeing through my soul. *Oh, he was a freak!*

While he caressed my toes with his tongue, my head dropped back as my eyes rolled to the back of my head. I began to strip my blazer and top off, exposing my red lace bra. He stepped back and pulled my cargo pants off my legs, then bit his bottom lip at the matching panties. Aaliyah made sure I was prepared for this tonight, or else my granny panties would've made an appearance.

Scooting up to the edge of the bed, I wrestled with his pants to expose his massive length as it sprang up in my face. It was only right to taste the bead of precum that eased out. He lay his head back and groaned as I took it in as much as I could. Lucien reached down and tangled his fingers in my tresses.

He enjoyed every second as he began to pump slightly into my mouth. The little growls fueled my pursuit to have him come unglued. He slid back from me, then bent to kiss the mess I was making from my mouth.

"I can't let you take me out like that. I want you on your knees, ass up in the air."

I didn't hesitate to follow directions when the bed dipped, followed by a warm, wet feeling between my cheeks. He feasted until I shivered beneath him. Sliding inside slowly, he paused to allow us both time to soak in the feeling. The moans and whimpers I tried to hide in the pillow were cut short when he leaned over and whispered in my ear, "Let me hear that shit. Don't be shy now."

With a loud smack, he increased his tempo of the in and out motion. He leaned over again and pressed his weight on my back until I was flat on the mattress with his arm around my neck while he slowly stroked it. He whispered in my ear as he stroked me to oblivion.

"You know you are mine, right?"

The words were caught in my brain but wouldn't translate to my mouth. Moaning was the only option.

"No more running from me. Understand?"

"Y-yes!"

"I don't know why you were running, but we can work through all that. You hear me. I got you. You look so pretty taking all of me." The words he spoke in my ear and the things he made me feel had tears running down my face. His hand reached under me and flicked my nub until I was sobbing and trembling in his arms. He buried his face in my neck, sucked and stroked until his body stiffened and his release came to an end.

We lay there catching our breath before he left to take care of his hygiene. He came back with a basket ready to complete the aftercare. The cold bottle of water and warm, wet towel were a thoughtful gesture to end one of the greatest sexual experiences I have had.

Lying in bed under his considerably large arm, I drifted off to sleep peacefully. His scent was soothing me and my panther into a deep state of slumber. Suddenly, Lucien's scent turned acrid, and my eyes flew open.

The room was pitch black, but I could see his face was contorted in anguish, his lips trembled, and his heart rate increased to a rapid pace. He must have been having a nightmare. The night was still young, so he wasn't too deep in it yet, so I shook him awake.

Sitting up, he turned on a lamp on his nightstand. The confused look on his face told me he was unaware of what was happening in his body.

"Baby, you were having a nightmare. What were you dreaming about?"

He blew out a deep breath and wiped his hand down his face. "Sometimes, I replay the events of my sister being kidnapped or my time in the military. It's hyper realistic and feels like I'm back in that time."

"Does this happen often?"

"Not all the time. Sometimes, things in life happen that trigger a memory of my sister or something."

"You can't keep on like that, though. It sounds like Post Traumatic Stress Disorder- PTSD. Have you seen someone about it?" Concern was laced in my tone as I questioned him.

"Briefly, when I left the military. It was a requirement. But look, don't worry about it. I'm good." He tried to brush it off as if it was nothing, but I could hear his heart rate increase in my sleep.

With my eyebrows drawn together, I asked, "So you have been dealing with this alone? For years?" I was pissed that he didn't use his own resources that he offered to families. Therapy was instrumental in healing from such a traumatic experience. The loss of a sibling is major. A twin.

"Besides my mom, my ex knows about it. The ex was scared I would kill her in her sleep. Said she didn't want a crazy man."

That shit broke my heart and pissed my panther off. She wanted to go out and find her to rip her head smooth off her shoulders. She came to the surface as we looked at Lucien.

"It's time to go back to therapy. You just told me WE would get through what I was going through earlier." I waved my hands between the two of us. "It's the same thing for you. I got you, too."

He stared at me like I hung the moon and the stars. Apparently, he didn't experience genuine concern outside of his mom. My big baby needed love, too. He created a foundation to help everyone affected by trafficking and forgot about himself in the process.

Lying back in the bed, he wrapped himself around my body as we both drifted back to sleep. My panther was anxious for blood. She whispered to me that Lucien was our mate. She had faith he would accept us both.

The acrid scent woke me again, but this time his body was wracked with tremors. Getting up from under him, I straddled his body using my body weight to help ground him. I whispered positive affirmations in his ear as he slept to reinforce my earlier words. He wouldn't be alone. He would get through this, and I would be by his side.

As I lay on him, my panther purred in his ear to calm his slight jerking movements. Panthers use the slight rumble and chest vibrations from the purring noise to soothe their mate. She had already claimed him as hers, and a bitch better watch it with him.

Chapter 10

Lucien

Saturday morning hit a little different as I woke up just how I pictured it, Keisha on my chest and her hair splayed out in my bed. Her golden-brown skin glowed under the sunlight. Her body covered in my scent, her neck marked by my lips made me smile. She had me out here feeling like a teenaged boy.

Jumping up out of her sleep, Keisha ran to the restroom then started dressing. "Shit! I missed a family...thing."

I looked at her with a raised eyebrow. What kind of...thing was her family into? She was hiding something but we were still new so I wouldn't press her. I knew almost everything there was to know about her family so I wasn't too worried.

"Well, babe, get dressed and I'll drop you off at home. We can link up later this afternoon."

In the car, Keisha had pulled her hair into a high ponytail. I preferred it to be wild and loose like when we met. She can get all glammed up but her natural state was the prettiest to me. I pulled that white ghost into her driveway and walked her to the door. Before leaving I made sure to get one last taste of her.

She turned to me abruptly at the door and said, "Do you have any plans for tomorrow? I want you to come meet my family."

I stood there like a deer caught in headlights. Shit! I see she was taking us serious and don't get me wrong, I was glad. I just didn't think this far. Knowing it was about to be some shit, I put on my game face and replied, "Sure let me know what time I need to be here to pick you up."

Kissing her lips one more time, I turned back and headed to my car to figure this shit out. I know her dad and Jamilah were going to recognize me as soon as I walked in the door. I just hope they didn't put my business out there before I got a chance too.

Maybe I should tell her now to get it over with. I didn't want to ruin what we had going, hell, it just started. As I drove back to the house, last night was heavy on my mind. I couldn't let all that get away from me.

Baby was dressed nice for us to be just going to a family Sunday dinner. She even put on makeup. Her curls were more curly and pulled into an updo and she wore a gorgeous sundress with them pretty toes out. I might develop a fetish because of those toes.

Using my military training, I leveled my breathing out as we walked up to her family home. I needed to steady my heartbeat and get my game face on. She turned to look at me then tilted her head to the side. Like she could sense my nervousness. She probably thought I was just anxious about meeting her parents but there were a few things she didn't know about me.

Our hands intwined as we walked through the moderately decorated home to the dining area. Everyone was just being seated at the table. "Hey guys! I want you to meet my boyfriend, Lucien."

Everyone looked up or turned their heads in my direction. The first pair of eyes to meet mine were Jamilah's. They were the biggest pair of eyes at the table. I saw Xavier knee Nia under the table but she was clueless as to who I was. No one said anything but the looks around the table told a million stories. Keisha was oblivious to the stares and the side eye I was receiving from them throughout dinner.

"So, Lucien, what is it that you do?" Keisha's mom, Shirley, asked.

"Here we go!" Jamilah said dramatically, picked up her wine and pushed her chair back a little from the table then crossed her legs. All eyes looked at her and a few of the sisters giggled under their breath.

"I am the CEO of a nonprofit organization that helps victims and family of trafficking." Putting a little more base in my voice as I spoke to Keisha's mother. She had been a lot quieter than I expected. Keisha told me she gave Nia's fiancé a hard time their first dinner. She didn't think he was good enough for her and wanted her with a doctor or someone more stable financially.

"That's so noble of you," she said uninterested then turned to Keisha's dad, the man I knew as Timothy and asked, "Do you need anything else, baby?" Kind of odd. I'll have to ask about that later. He just shook his head no and kept watching me.

Dinner was mild compared to what I figured would happen. Most of the conversation came from Keisha and her sisters. Afterward, the men retired to Timothy's movie room while the women gossiped more and cleaned the dining room and kitchen.

I walked in his movie room, ready for the smoke. Timothy sat in a recliner watching a basketball game with a glass of Old Fashioned in his hand. He sat up when I walked in but before he could open his mouth to say anything Jamilah busted in the room.

Xavier, Timothy and I all watched as she walked in, sat on the couch and crossed her legs. She was extremely dramatic. Addressing the elephant in the room I started, "Look I-."

"You better not be trying to play my sister to get closer to one of your targets," Jamilah interrupted me as I was about to inform them I wasn't on anything funny.

"Man, I'm not on anything like that. I met her that day we were talking outside of Lucky's, remember? I have no ulterior motives. I genuinely like her."

Crossing her arms she stood up and said "Mmhmm," then walked out. I guess my answer was sufficient for her.

Looking at Xavier and Timothy, I could tell Xavier was still a little salty about how we met. Not my fault his daddy was a bitch in the wrong place. Timothy sat back and continued to watch the game.

Sitting on the couch to watch the game, he raised his glass to take a sip then said, "You need to tell her. Tonight! We are very much a like when it comes to our careers but if you hurt my babygirl like that last mu'fucka, I'll kill you."

He sat back and we finished watching the game in silence. Xavier never said a word to me the rest of the night. I did remember my goons at the warehouse did him dirty. We left shortly after the game ended. The dark of night glowed through the car windows and the moonlight glowed on Keisha's skin.

A relief washed over me as we walked into her home. I wasn't under a microscope anymore. I just needed to come clean. As Keisha changed out her clothes into something more comfortable, I paced the living room floor. I killed people for a living, talking to her shouldn't be an issue.

"We need to talk," I blurted out as soon as she walked into the living room. Her face was marred with confusion as she folded her legs underneath her body on the couch. She sat and waited for me to continue. This shit was stupid. She was a cop working on cases where I was the damn perpetrator. She might try to arrest my ass right here.

"I haven't been completely honest about what I do for a living." The look of defeat crossed her face briefly before she schooled her expression. "Yes, I do have a non-profit for victims but...I also have a business to eradicate the threats that risk the safety of Blackwater residents."

She sat on the couch, legs crossed looking as I talked. Silence filled the room for several minutes as she worked out this new information in her head. The tension in the air was almost unbearable. I had to tell her the full story of how I knew some of her family, too.

"I took an oath to serve and protect the citizens in Blackwater. I take that serious, Lucien. This can't work."

"You would still be protecting the community, Shadow comes out when things need to be corrected." Walking to the couch I kneeled to eye level with her. "This is no different than your dad. Things with Shadow would stay away from you."

Looking in her eyes, I hoped my words were easing her racing mind.

Since we met, she had become an important person that I wouldn't want to lose. Now that we had crossed that line the other night, we wouldn't be apart. If she needed time, I would give her that but we were going to be together.

"So is that who you are during that time? Shadow?"

"Yes. It was a name I got in the military. Once you saw me it was too late but I was always around. Hiding in the shadows."

"Wait, was that you? My cases?" she said folding her arms. Shaking her head, she talked to herself while pacing the living room floor.

I didn't even bother to answer. She knew. Stopping in front of me, she stared down in my face. "Is that why you pursued me? I could keep what you do a secret? You men are all the same. Always trying to use and manipulate women." She turned to walk away.

Before she could get far, I jumped up and grabbed her arm. "Of course not. I didn't expect for you to be a total vibe. I was drawn to you but didn't expect it to go past the first date. Hell, I was hoping you were crazy or shallow so I could walk away from your ass."

"I think you should leave Lucien. You lied and tried to play in my face." She was pacing and talking to herself out loud like someone was answering. She whispered to herself. "Clearly this isn't what we thought it was." Wrapping her hands around her body, when I looked into her face I saw a glimmer of blue in her eyes.

This was an untamed anger I hadn't seen before with her. She was visibly shaking. Normally, I didn't give a fuck about someone being mad at me but this was different. Keisha was different.

"I want you out, Lucien. I need more time to think."

Walking up on her, I tilted my head to the side. I needed to read what was going on behind her eyes. This was more than what she was saying out loud. She was using this as another opportunity to run from me.

"You want me out? For doing the same thing your family is into?"

Raising her chin in the air, she folded her arms across her chest and said sternly, "I want you out because you lied to me. How long were you going to keep this a secret? Until I put it all together? Until I lost my job, being connected to you? Or until you were done with me, got what you wanted, and no longer needed me?" Her voice elevated and trembled at the end.

My eyebrows scrunched up at her words. Her ex must have been horrible. I saw what it was now. That "man before me syndrome" had a hold on her, and she was treating me like I was him. Like, there was a history of lies and manipulation from me.

Lowering my voice and taking a deep breath, I needed to be the calm one in this situation. She was hurt, and lashing out at me was all she could do right now.

"I'm going to give you your space tonight." I stepped closer into her space, and she stood her ground, not flinching. "I'm not walking away, and neither are you. Sleep on it tonight, and I will see you tomorrow." Kissing her forehead, I turned and walked out of her house.

Turning to close her door, I saw she still stood in the living room, stunned. She may be used to an emotional man arguing back and forth with her but that was not me. I'd give her tonight to clear her head.

Chapter 11

Keisha

Tossing and turning all night, my spirit was deeply disturbed. Then my panther wouldn't shut up all night, whining. She wanted Lucien with us. His commanding nature had her wrapped around his finger. As an apex predator, my panther enjoyed the safety and comfort that Lucien brought.

I struggled to reconcile the oath that I took with Shadow, the man my heart was falling for. Today would be difficult with my mind bogged down with thoughts of him and my body needing sleep. The dreary weather didn't help my mood either, there was no sun out to give me that boost of serotonin I needed.

Walking into the precinct, I was the center of attention, as usual, with my wild curls and my black pantsuit. My office light splayed bright, causing me to roll my eyes because I was not in the mood for the newbie and his questions.

"Good morning, Carter! You're here early." As I walked in the door hesitantly, I noticed he jumped from the cabinet he was looking in when I came into the office. My panther felt something was off with him and went on high alert. What could he have been looking for? The cabinet wasn't off limits, but he responded like a kid caught with his hand in the cookie jar. Odd.

"Uh, good morning, Detective Grant! How is it going?"

I kept to my desk as if I were unaware of his weird behavior. I had bigger fish to fry than to worry about what the newbie had going on. Pulling out my phone, I opened the group chat with my sisters.

Me: So everyone knew and said nothing to me. WTF?!

Jamilah responded with the eyeball emojis.

Me: Don't play dumb, Milah. Everyone knew about Shadow but me.

Aaliyah: Who is Shadow?

Nia: I just found out who he was Sunday night after dinner. X told me on the drive home.

Milah: I didn't think the mystery man would be Shadow. That man was scary when I first met him. I didn't think his mean ass would have a girlfriend.

Me: I'm not his girlfriend. I broke it off last night when he told me about his extracurricular activities.

Milah: Girl, why? You must be on them good drugs. That man is fine.

Me: He lied to me, Milah. Then let's not act like he isn't involved in some stuff that is the complete opposite of my career. I took an oath.

Milah: Girl, be so for real right now. You forgot you were on payroll for the Onyx Hunt. You're delusional.

Aaliyah: Wait! Who is Shadow?

Rolling my eyes, I closed the group chat. I was done with their asses. Of all times, Jamilah wanted to be sensible today, and my poor twin was so clueless. Putting my phone in my pocket, I needed to jump back into work and focus on my cases. As I looked up, Carter was watching me, but turned his head right as I locked eyes with him.

Now that my cases were actually solved, I needed to make sure Carter's nosey ass didn't overstep. He has been really interested in the victims and the evidence left at the scene on their personal lives. We worked in silence until I decided to take a lunch break. I needed to call Lucien to make this right.

Needing a minute outside of the station, I sat in my car to make the call. The rain finally started, causing my hair to puff more and grow substantially. The phone rang twice before he picked up, but he didn't say anything.

"Have you eaten? Let me take you to lunch."

A loud, boisterous laugh rang out on the phone. "Hey, baby. No, I haven't eaten yet. Come get me so we can go pick something up." Instantly, my mood changed as I whipped out of the parking lot. Pulling up to his company about twenty minutes later, I hopped out, ready to see my fine ass man.

I thought about what Jamilah said in the group chat all morning, and she was right. I was being delusional. I actively helped my dad with the Onyx Hunt in whatever way he needed me. Having my panther riding me tough helped me make the decision to stop being stubborn. My panther was howling inside from excitement that I was going to get her man.

Lucien met me at the front door to the lobby, grabbing my face to kiss my lips. He wasn't worried about who saw our make-out session either. The world around us melted away as he sucked my tongue, causing me to moan in his mouth as he pulled away. He put his forehead to mine as he looked in my eyes.

"I knew I would see your crazy ass. If you didn't call me, I was pulling up later. I told you no more running from me," he said as he stared into my soul. The rigidity throughout his body told me he meant business.

"Yes, sir, Mr. Shadow, sir!" I mocked and gave him a fake salute.

He gave me a humorless laugh, then leaned in closer to my ear and practically growled, "You call me Lucien or baby. I'll even accept Daddy." He smirked, looking down into my face, "but don't call me Shadow. You don't know him."

That should have made me feel nervous, but his demeanor and tone got my juices flowing. Lucien was a six-foot-five-inch chocolate boss in every sense of the word. Being patient seemed to be a skill not extended to many other people, but to me and his mom. He grabbed my hand and led me to the car so we could get lunch.

As big as my car was, Lucien still seemed cramped in the front seat. Even though I drove this time, he still came and opened my door when we pulled up to Lucky's Wingspot. The parking lot was across the street from the restaurant, and Lucien made sure to grab my hand to guide me across safely. He kept his eyes open, watching our surroundings. I guess it was years of military training that kept him diligent in safety. His hand never left my body until we sat at our table.

Sitting across from him, the feeling of weightlessness in my spirit confirmed this was where I needed to be. Unlike with Wilton, I was free to rest in the moment. Not on guard, anxious about whether he was happy. Now, if I could just get him to stop calling me. Speaking of, my cell phone rang at the table.

As I silenced the call, Lucien looked over at it and said, "You can take your call, baby." There was a slight lift in his eyebrow as he watched me tense at the sight of Wilton's name. Biting the side of my lip, I shook my leg as I tried to broach this subject with Lucien. We haven't talked about exes yet.

"It's ok. Wilton is my ex who doesn't quit. No matter how many times I tell him we aren't getting back together." He sat there quietly, taking it all in while I talked. Simple. Then there was a dark chuckle. Kind of ominous. Was this Shadow showing himself? "What's that laugh about?"

"Homeboy better find something safe to do before he finds himself somewhere stinking. Let him know next time he calls. Your man's not about to play those games with him."

Oh snap! I think I like Shadow. We ordered our food and drinks. Then he hit me with a big question I wasn't ready for. I thought us talking about my ex was over, especially since I didn't really want to talk or even think about Wilton.

"What happened to end your relationship?" A simple question that had the potential to uncover so many scars, expose insecurities, and possibly end my good mood.

Sitting up straighter in my seat, I sucked in a deep breath before my mind ventured back down memory lane to such a disaster. "I thought I was in love with someone I wanted to spend the rest of my life with, but turns out I was just comfortable." Pausing, I thought about all of the conversations with my sister and how she helped me come to that conclusion when I finally decided to listen to her.

"He didn't really like me, he just liked the idea of me. What having me represented for him. There was plenty of red flags, and I repainted them the color I wanted them to be. He made me forget who I was, accept things I would never, and I promised myself to never go back." It took everything out of me to keep my composure.

I have worked hard to move past that relationship and the damage it caused me and my self-esteem. I let this man put his hands on me a few times when I could have easily snatched his throat out with my claws. My panther stopped trusting me until we finally left that situation. The person I had become was stronger and a work in progress. Honestly, I was glad for Lucien's patience with me because trust was not given freely in my world.

Lucien sat and watched as I processed my feelings. His face twitched as I continued. "He played a lot of mind games. He ever put his hands on you?" At that moment, I knew I couldn't lie. He watched too hard. He was too observant. I fought hard not to fidget. Not breathe. His facial expression told me he already knew before I could even answer. His jaw tightened before he spoke.

"You know you're safe over here. No mind games. I'll only put my hands on you when I'm smacking that ass as you throw it back." He looked at me with low eyes and a devious grin on his face. At that moment, the tension I felt was released from my shoulders. I threw my head back in laughter. His attempt to lighten the mood worked, but it also piqued my curiosity.

"That's enough about me and my bullshit ex. Your birthday is coming on Friday. You only have four more days. What are your plans?" I asked enthusiastically. He just sat and smirked.

"I don't really do much for my birthday. Without Lisette, things don't feel right. I'm out here turning up celebrating life, and she is God-knows-where, just don't sit right with me."

"I can't tell you I understand how you feel, but I do know that you deserve to celebrate yourself. You are successful. You are still alive, and that means a lot, to me, especially. I'm happy that you are here." Looking into his eyes, I hoped he felt all the emotions that I had behind my words. In a short period of time, I have felt more for this man than I ever did for my ex.

The way that he was a rider for his sister made my heart swell for him and cry at the same time. I was determined to help him find her, or at least help with dismantling trafficking organizations with him.

Now that we decided to move forward with our relationship, I was all in with him. Lucien's heart was pure, and he showed me every time we were together. I needed to keep Carter far away from uncovering anything about my man.

"I hear you. Let's just go on a date. We can end our night watching movies at my house. Is that good enough?" He had the nerve to look annoyed that I wanted to celebrate his ass. I got something for him.

"I got you, baby. I can end the night under you." His face changed then. "Uh huh! I thought you would change your tone." We both laughed as we headed out of Lucky's. Again, he was so gentle with me, getting back to my car and opening the door for me.

We pulled up to his office, and he invited me into check things out. His office building wasn't the only business inside. There looked to be two or three other companies sharing the five-story office structure. The mostly glass office building was really upscale.

The decor was top-notch, the smell was very inviting, and even the carpet was upgraded to a more plush feel under your feet. Before we made it to his suite, I had to stop at the ladies room. "Babe, I need to stop in the restroom. I'll meet you at your suite."

He nodded and strutted toward the door of his suite. As I headed in the direction of the ladies' room, two interesting-looking guys came down the hall discussing something important. The stranger closest to me didn't even look up as we got closer and ran into me, slamming my body into the wall.

I scoffed as my body bounced off the wall with a loud thud. He turned his head to look at me, then nastily stated, "You should watch where you're going. You could get hurt out here." I rolled my eyes and was about to pull my detective card on his ass when a big figure swooped in front of me, yanking the man who shoved me up against the wall by his throat.

My heart beat out of my chest with how fast he moved. He was talking in a low tone, but my panther hearing picked up on the threat. “Motherfucker you thought you would come in here and put your hands on this woman. My woman. You fucked up today.” The angry look on their faces told me things wouldn’t just end with a threat.

“Oh, since you fucking her its a problem? Just save some for my turn.” As those words left his mouth, the growl from Lucien's throat seemed to have powered the strength behind him, launching that man down the hallway. His friend tried to jump in to defend him and ended up being knocked out. As blood gushed from his nose, Lucien walked to the other one lying on the ground and dragged him to lie beside his friend.

Turning to me, he checked to see if I was ok, then pulled me into a hug. He had no idea I could take care of myself with those two. He pulled out his phone to call security to wrangle them up and kick them off the premises.

They were partners at an accounting firm upstairs, and this incident led to the entire business to be evicted from the building. Lucien called his lawyer and sent them the security footage just in case they wanted to come back with a lawsuit.

Shadow was highly protective, but I loved every bit of it. My panther was pleased at his display of dominance during that altercation. We were able to sit back and watch a real one go to work for us.

“You are coming to my house tonight. Give me a few minutes to get my things. Then follow me home.”

"But I don't have any clothes at your house. I need to go home."

"I'll give you my black card, you can order what you need. You need some stuff at my house anyway."

Standing there with my mouth open, he grabbed my hand and led me into his office to gather his things. He wasn't all talk but all action, and he was going to have to pry me off him with a crowbar tonight.

Chapter 12

Lucien

That little altercation with Keisha and that man had my blood pressure high. I turned around to let her know the suite number to come to when I heard everything that had happened around the corner. The sound of her body colliding with the wall had me seeing red. I almost caught a body on Candid Camera.

Ever since Má confirmed that she was the one, it's been all gas, no brakes in my pursuit of her. The journey of getting to know each other has been intense, but I wouldn't have it any other way. As she lay on my side with her silk nighty on, I soaked in the smell of her hair as we fell asleep.

The next morning, the sweet aroma of breakfast and coffee hit my nose and jolted me out of my sleep. With just my pajama pants on, I dragged myself to the bathroom to get my day started right and took care of my hygiene. Making my way to the kitchen, my heart stopped at the sight before me.

Keisha's beautiful bronze skin illuminated under the sunlight as she made our plates with just some black boy shorts on and a black see-through camisole that showed her chocolate-covered areolas. My mouth watered at the scene as my pajama pants tightened around my hips. Her hair was wild and curly. We both loved that free look and feel.

She tied her hair up before we lay in the bed, but I couldn't help but run my fingers through it as we made a mess of the sheets last night. I'm surprised she had enough energy to get up early to make breakfast after all of our sessions. Her vocal cords needed time to recover from whining out my name all night.

That hotbox was just too good to stay out of, and I had no plans to. Especially after that shit with those guys at my building. Another man putting their hands on my woman will never be accepted. If I weren't tied up last night, I would have gone to pay some people a few visits. I'll see them in due time, though.

Walking behind her, I wrapped my arms around Keisha and pushed my face in the crook of her neck to inhale heaven. The shit just fit and calmed my spirit. "Good morning! You got it smelling good in here."

"Good morning! I can't stay long. I need to get to the office early. I have a new partner that's kind of nosey. He has been sneaking and snooping. I don't trust it, so I need to stay a few steps ahead."

Going around the kitchen island, I pulled out my barstool to sit and eat. I just shook my head in understanding. *I need to look into him when I get to the office.* "You said he was new. What's his name?" I looked up from my plate, waiting for her response to my question. She hesitated giving up his name like I was going to kill the man.

"What? I just want to look into him. I'm not going to do anything to that man." I just laughed at her. *She thinks she knows me. She does though.* I wouldn't do anything to put her or her career in jeopardy. This woman came into my life and shook shit up real quick. Couldn't mess that up.

"His name is Carter Vincent. Leave that damn man alone, Lucien." She leaned in, kissed me on the lips, then cleaned her mess in the kitchen. She pranced out of the kitchen to get dressed for work, and I hated to see her go, but I loved to watch her leave. When she came back in she returned with her signature high bun and a black pantsuit. Simple. Sexy. Too sexy. I might have to pop up.

Walking into my office, I passed by my full-length mirror on my closet door. I had to admit I wasn't a slouch either. I looked good, and I felt even better. Last night's sessions sucked the stress right out of my body. Now, on to look up this partner. Being in the Special Forces, I was assigned to the intelligence support division and learned more than how to be a shadow. I was enriched with the knowledge to track down just about anyone who had a paper trail.

That was partly the reason I believed Lisette wasn't alive. I couldn't find her anywhere on the map. She just vanished like a ghost. Calling in the reinforcements, Jamilah Grant was supposed to be the bridge I obtained to get the info I needed. She was tough with hacking and tracking, but the Onyx Hunt secured her talents. I understood her wanting to stay with the family business.

Obtaining information on Carter Vincent should be as easy as taking candy from a baby. I went through my usual search and saw exactly how the rookie ended up in the position to be partnered with a high-ranking detective, Nepotism. His Uncle was an upper-level captain with the department. The whole family was connected with law enforcement in some way. A few more clicks opened Pandora's Box to the jackpot. Carter Vincent and his uncles were connected with the cover-up of a few cases. Some cases never made it to the investigation stage because of them. He must have been placed with her to keep her from making any discoveries. If Keisha found out anything about the trafficking, that would put her life in danger.

Not if I got to his ass first. They got the wrong one. I could catch him this weekend. It looks like he was a member at a local gym. That was the perfect setup for me to get in and out without being spotted. Taking care of this issue for my baby would be the perfect birthday gift to myself.

Switching gears, I needed to work on housing opportunities for my new project, Lis House. It would be a recovery house for women with little to no family to support them getting back on their feet. This was another way I could honor my sister.

Má was right, I needed to live my life. Keisha was a bright light in my darkness, outlined with thoughts of my sister. She let her walls down for me, and that meant a lot. All three of those women could get whatever they wanted from me with no hassle.

The workday went on without a word from Keisha. No calls or texts, which wasn't like her. She didn't even return the calls or texts I sent. My mind was tired from the work of today. Writing grants, looking at blueprints, and finalizing plans took a toll on me. I needed to head home and climb in my bed. Walking to my car, I was determined to find out where my baby was after yet another call was ignored.

The sun was descending from the sky, leaving a purple and orange hue in its wake. The sunsets in Blackwater were beautiful and put me in the mood to sit and watch them fade to darkness. Driving by her house, I didn't see any movement at her residence. That was a major problem I needed to rectify.

Pulling up to my home, the place was pitch black, just like I liked it. There was no movement. No sound. Just darkness. What I needed to get in the right headspace for Shadow. The attire for the night was Shadow's typical all-black, cargo pants, and hoodie.

Jumping in my matte black truck, I was off to canvas the small town for Ms. Keisha. She'd better have a good reason for not calling me back today. I was low-key having withdrawals. Her detective work was no excuse for not responding. I needed to know she was ok.

Creeping down the block of a dark neighborhood, I saw the infamous cobalt blue Audi parked in an alley. "Man, what the fuck is going on?" I couldn't believe my eyes. My heart raced as my brain came to the realization that the car belonged to Keisha.

The night was dark, the streets were quiet, and a slight fog was in the air. I could make out two figures standing and talking. Her normally unruly hair was tucked away in a low ponytail, and the only way I could identify her was from the slight illumination from the streetlights.

Pulling my truck to the side, I cut out all my lights. I turned off my truck, then sat quietly to watch and listen as much as possible. She stood face to face with what looked to be a man. Their positions and body language told me they were familiar with each other, but there was no ill intent. Relaxed but mindful.

Her face focused intently on what the stranger was saying. Something about the commissioner from her case. The stranger must be a CI, Confidential Informant, helping her with the case.

Shit! That's why Carter was sent to be her partner. *She must be getting close to something to follow a lead so intently. She already knew who the killer was, so why continue to follow up on that case?* Keisha kept her eyes all around, surveying her surroundings. That made my heart proud that my baby knew how to handle herself out here in these streets.

Suddenly, her back went straight as she raised her hand to pause the conversation with the man she was meeting with. A figure stepped out of the shadows, but I couldn't make out a face. I could make out a gun in his hand though. My body moved faster than my brain recognized, and I was out of the truck.

The chill in the air cut through the thickness of my hoodie and had the hair on my neck standing straight up. My heart beating out of my chest was the loudest sound surrounding me. A cold sweat came over me as I thought about what the unknown man was here to do. Stealthily, I ran up to be closer to the action in case things went south.

"Keisha, what are you doing? You couldn't just mind your business." The unknown man said in a fake deep voice as he walked closer to Keisha and her CI. He projected fake confidence, but I could hear the hoe in his voice. She stood stock still as the new person walked up to them. Her eyes shone with familiarity when the new person stepped into the light.

"Carter? What are you doing here?" Her eyebrows knitted together as her eyes dropped to his hand holding a gun at his waist. She looked taken aback at his actions. Moving in front of her CI, she told him to run. As she walked to Carter, his movements became fidgety. Anxious. Rocking from side to side then raised his gun.

She raised her hands in surrender, then calmly said, "What is this about? We can figure this out. Put the gun down." Not scared. Just rage contained. Her movements were slow and careful. I waited in a dark nook, watching everything play out. She could handle herself, but we locked in, and I would always have her back.

"Bitch, you just had to try to be a hero. You had to keep digging deeper. This is bigger than you could imagine." His eyes grew wilder as he waved the gun at her. His other hand combed through his oily blonde hair as sweat ran down his face. "Bigger than this little ass town. So the big boys sent me to take care of you." Her eyes grew wider, and that hint of blue she always carried seemed to grow larger. He pulled back and swung the gun at her. The metal swiped across her cheek as she staggered.

Instantly, her body shifted into the largest feline I had ever seen up close. All black with vibrant cobalt-blue eyes. She lunged at his neck as he raised his gun. A deafening shot rang out into the night. Loud, ear-piercing shrieks could be heard for miles, but... it was a males voice. As I ran to her aid, the blur of claws thwarted my vision. My eyes were met with an unsightly mangled body. Keisha stood before me, blood-soaked, half-naked, and shaking.

Blood dripped from her hands and mouth as she stared into my eyes. Shock covered her face, and another emotion. Was it...shame?

Chapter 13

Keisha

This is all bad. How much did he see? Shock flooded my nervous system as Lucien walked up and grabbed me in a hug. He used his body to cover my sight from the maimed figure lying lifeless on the cold asphalt. My body shook, waiting for the moment his brain caught up with reality. I wasn't ready for him to know and definitely didn't want it to come out like this.

"I got you, baby. Let me go to my truck and get you a blanket," he whispered. As he jogged back, I was stunned by his actions. He hadn't mentioned my panther at all. As shocking as it was, my panther whined at him, ignoring her presence. I knew I had to be the one to broach this topic.

Grabbing the blanket, he draped it around my shoulders. I looked up to him and said, "We need to talk about what you just saw. I know you have que—."

He started shaking his head as he hugged me tighter. "I don't have any questions. I know your family are panther shifters. You don't grow up in Bayou Grisé, Louisiana, with a magical family and not see a thing or two." Taking the blanket, he tried to wipe some of the blood from my face. Looking down in my face, he said, "Here is the story you need to go with. You and your partner were set to meet your CI, but he was running late. As you were standing in the alley talking, a large animal attacked. You were able to scare it away, but not before it viciously attacked your partner. Sound good?"

I tilted my head to the side at this man. Not only was he not phased by my panther, but he was giving me a cover story to protect us. My panther was no longer jealous of his ignoring her presence but purring at his protecting of us. She came to the surface and wanted to shift right then to be with him, but I fought to keep her inside.

"My panther is anxious to meet you. How did you know?"

"Remember, I worked with Jamilah very briefly, and I always do my homework on the people I deal with." We walked back to my car when I called my sergeant to let him know what happened with Carter. Lucien and I stood and waited for the entire department to show up due to Carter's death.

"Am I a bad person for feeling free from having him attached to my side?" I looked over to Lucien and asked. He was going to try to kill me, but I still feel like I should feel more about his death.

"Don't. He was in on the trafficking ring. Hell, there are a few of them in this police department tied into this mess. So keep it to yourself. I had been trying to reach you all day to let you know. I had to find you when I hadn't heard from you."

This new information ran me hotter than fish grease. How were we supposed to be the ones here to serve and protect, but there were some only here to prey and collect. I rushed to the trunk of my vehicle to change into some spare clothes. When we shift, the transition destroys them, and I didn't want to raise any questions. We sat on the hood of my car and waited as several police vehicles pulled in the alley. Men hopped out of their vehicles and marched to the scene. I straightened my back and put on my detective face to deal with the aftermath. EMS pulled in shortly after, thank God, to give me a little reprieve from the hard stares and questions.

"Who is this, Grant?" My Sergeant said with a stern voice and a hard look on his face.

"This is my boyfriend, Lucien. He was in the area when I called him, so he came to check on me." Lucien never moved off the hood of my car but kept his head down and looked his eyes at the man. I could see Shadow wanted to show his face. He didn't trust any of them.

"He just so happened to be in the area, huh?" he said suspiciously. He also didn't try to introduce himself. Now, everyone was a suspect in my head. Lucien told me that this whole trafficking thing went beyond Carter. Now Carter's words were making sense.

Bitch, you just had to try to be a hero. You had to keep digging deeper. This is bigger than you could imagine. Bigger than this little ass town. So the big boys sent me to take care of you.

They sent him to kill me. So was this all a setup? Bringing him in as my partner to watch me?

Was my sergeant in on it? At this point, I couldn't trust anyone. It was just Lucien and me in this fight now. "You can go home now, baby. I know I have a lot of questions to answer."

"I'll wait right here until you are done. Remember what we talked about." He reached over to kiss my lips and made me do a handshake that I made him learn. People from the department were standing around watching, but Lucien didn't care. I know it was his way of saying we were locked in, and that made me feel invincible.

Hostility rolled off the guys as I passed each one with my head held high. Street cops, detectives, and other higher-ranking officers stood around watching my every move. I watched them all just as hard now. Everyone was a suspect.

After the questioning was done, I walked back to Lucien, who was right where he said he would be. My sergeant met me at the car and said, "Grant, take off tomorrow to recover. Sorry you had to deal with this tonight. Get some rest!" He reached out to pat me on the shoulder, then turned to walk away.

Lucien's house was the only place I wanted to be last night. Waking up in his home always felt right. The bright sun blazed through his bedroom window, waking me from the deep sleep his bed put me in. His bed was huge and had the softest comforter ever. After my shower last night, it guided me right to sleep.

Taking the day off felt foreign, but I was definitely going to enjoy my time. I made an appointment with my favorite sister, and we were headed to lunch at Lucky's. The bar that has seen the Grants a lot through the years. We go there to laugh, cry, and gossip about our lives. It's our place to catch a game and eat wings or sit in a booth and have a chill date. The owner was also a shifter, so if anything happened there, we knew he would take care of it, keeping our identity hidden. Shifters were kept an underground secret here in Blackwater.

Walking into Lucky's, I looped my arm around my twins as we pranced to our usual table. The Wingspot was almost empty, which was perfect for gossiping. No possible ears overhearing the wrong thing. I had so much to spill too.

"So how has work been?" I went right into our usual topics before we got to the juicy stuff.

"It's the same stuff, different day. Genesis and Omari have gotten serious. So I talk to her more now. She is really cool. Not so serious all the time now."

Nodding my head as I sipped my drink, I knew things were a little lighter in that building now. "That's good. Now that Genesis has a man, her uptight ass can channel some of that aggression on him. Have the break-ins calmed down at all?"

"Yes, girl. I think word got out with how she was putting heads through drywall, and it may have spooked a few people from taking the contracts." My head fell back in laughter at the Gargoyle kicking ass at my sister's library. "Enough about my job, how are things going at the PD? I heard there was some commotion the other night."

I rolled my eyes so hard, I'm surprised they didn't stick. "Girl, yes." I leaned in closer and lowered my voice to a whisper. "My partner tried to take me out, and a panther showed up to protect me. Unfortunately, he got the short end of the stick." I looked around the building to see if anyone could have been listening to our conversation.

Aaliyah sat there in shock as I recapped the night's events. She and I rarely shift into our panthers unless we are exercising or at our family run. So for my panther to come out, things must have gotten pretty crazy. "Then to top it all off, Lucien was lurking in the shadows like some kind of stalker."

She spat her water out in laughter at my description of him that night. The waiter brought our wings to the table, and we dived into our basket. She intensely listened as she ate her wings like she was in a movie theater. "Speaking of the crazy man..."

My phone rang on the table, and Lucien's picture flashed across my screen. "Hey, baby! What's up?"

His deep baritone voice rang through my phone's speaker as I held the phone up to my ear. “Hey! What are you doing? You sound busy.”

Smiling like a schoolgirl, I was happy to hear his voice. “Yeah, I’m with Aaliyah. We are up here getting something to eat at—” Just then, a tall figure approached our table. Aaliyah’s face twisted up in disgust, and her eyes glimmered a reddish pink color. Her panther was coming to the surface for some reason. As I looked over to see the guest at our table, I saw the reason for her disdain. Wilton.

“Keisha, can you hang up the phone? I need to talk to you.” He seemed frustrated, and his tone was short. Stunned at his audacity, my mouth just sat open as he demanded I get off the phone.

“Who the fuck is that?” Boomed in my ear, overstimulating me mentally.

Aaliyah read my face and jumped in to help. “Wilton, what do you want? Don’t you see she is on the phone?”

“I don’t give a damn who she's on the phone with. We need to talk.” He responded to her. “Keisha, get off the damn phone. What is this I hear about you having a boyfriend?”

“Tell Wilber to stay his ass right there.” A loud clack click followed by shuffling was heard in the background, a distinct sound I knew as him racking the slide of his gun. Shit!

“Wilton, say what you have to say, then leave. My personal business is none of your concern.” I rushed out before Lucien could say anything else in my ear. It got really quiet on his end too. I guess we all were listening to see what Wilton had to say.

"Keisha, we were supposed to be working on our relationship. How are you going to go and get a dude?"

"Y'all ain't working on shit!"

"Lucien! Stop yelling in my ear." He was pissed, apparently. Then the dinging sound of his truck could be heard from the phone's speaker.

"Wilton, there is nothing to work on. We are over and have been for a while. I have moved on and hope you do the same. Goodbye!" Hopefully, he took that as a hint to leave. I could imagine Shadow will be here shortly to cause hell.

"That's how it is? After everything we've been through? I'm not giving up on us that easy, Keisha. I'll be back. Hopefully, you come to your senses sooner rather than later." He turned and walked away. Aaliyah and I both looked at each other and shook our heads. I was still holding the phone to my ear as Lucien sat quietly on the other end.

"Hey, baby! You still there?" I prayed he had gone back home after he heard things were all good, but I knew better. This man probably had Wilton in the trunk of his car, tied up right now.

"Yeah, I'm here." His voice was tight and pained. "I was just calling to check on you. Does he pop up on you often?"

Damn! I didn't want to answer that. This wasn't going to help at all. "I can take care of myself, sir."

"That's not what I asked you. I know you can take care of yourself, but now you don't have to do it alone, ol' hard-headed ass woman. Stop deflecting and answer my question." His agitation at the situation could be heard in his voice. So now I'm getting in trouble, I was just an innocent bystander.

"He has come to a few of my crime scenes, but he doesn't approach me. Sometimes he will call or text me after, but I haven't seen him up close and personal in a while." He didn't respond, just a grunt to my answer. I didn't know what that meant but I was sure I would find out soon.

Ending the call, Aaliyah was enthralled in my drama-filled life with these men practically fighting for my attention. She looked like a chipmunk with her shoulders hunched, eating a wing, eyes bulging, watching me fight for my sanity between these two. "Girl, as much as I want everyone to get along, I was hoping Lucien popped up on Wilton's ass. I can't stand him."

"Definitely not. That would be a bad look for our family and me. You know Mama would have a heart attack." My mother cared about appearances and would never let me live it down if I had two men fighting over me. She would call them street hooligans. Even though it wouldn't be much of a fight with Lucien. Wilton's skinny ass didn't stand a chance.

We talked more about my drama and how I was worried about how deep this trafficking goes into my department. My sister was my best friend to whom I told everything. She sat and listened, but I saw the longing in her eyes for a true partner to do life with. First, it was Nia to find a mate, and now I'm happy with someone. She wasn't jealous, just waiting.

She wanted what most people wanted, her person. Other guys she dated were all liars who broke her heart. She was way too trusting with her heart. The sadness in her eyes betrayed the smile she put on for everyone.

When we left Lucky's, I knew I needed to be up under my man to get a feel for what was going through his head. Wilton wasn't worth getting his blood pressure up about. He was harmless, just annoying.

When I walked up to the pitch-black home, I knew Lucien was sitting in the dark watching TV like always. He opened the wooden glass door with just his pajama pants on. His muscular, tattooed chest on display made me lick my lips at his sexiness. I jumped on him, then wrapped my legs around his waist. He grabbed my duffel bag and led us into the house, while I buried my face in his neck to smell his signature cologne.

Chapter 14

Lucien

Walking out the door this morning, with a naked Keisha lying in my bed, was harder than morning wood. My drive into the office showed the beauty of the sun peeking through the clouds as it painted the sky hues of pink and orange. A stark contrast from what I was feeling inside.

I wanted to hunt. First on my agenda was to look up Wilton Cartwright. He couldn't be showing up to see my woman, pressing her about getting back with him. I could hear in his voice that he was going to be a problem. Dudes like him didn't give up until they got what they wanted.

Walking into my suite, Ms. Sharon was there to greet me as usual. Going over my agenda for the day, we walked into my office as I went to work looking up Wilton. Trust fund baby that had a full-ride scholarship to college. He had a promising basketball career, but then it just ended.

Did he get hurt? Why would anybody walk away from a career in the NBA? Oh well, something else would end soon if he keeps popping up on Keisha. My jaw tightened at the engagement announcement to Keisha and their photos. He still hadn't deleted them from his social media. This one photo of them sitting side by side at his family member's home, her eyes looked sad even with that fake smile plastered on her face.

Focused on my prey, I didn't hear the notification alert on my phone until it buzzed off the side of my desk. There was a text from Keisha. She was still off from Carter's death. Although I was happy it happened, I hated that she had to be the one to do it. Baby was fierce and didn't hesitate to put him down, just like her man. Swift action. No hesitation.

She wanted to go to dinner tonight to a new spot in Miramar Isle. Going online, I made the reservation for seven, then went back to investigating. I needed to know everything about Wilson since I would be seeing him soon.

Getting home, Keisha was getting ready for our date. She had some sexy R&B playing on the television while she dressed. Hair wild and free, just like I liked it, with one side pulled back to show her face. She pulled on a champagne, deep V-neck short dress. Her cleavage gave just enough to tease. I stood in the doorway, mesmerized by the masterpiece coming together. She then pulled out a shimmer lotion that made her bronze skin glisten with a golden shine. The gold accents she added finished the outfit perfectly. Somebody was getting fucked tonight.

Stalking her like a madman, she ignored my presence. “Don’t come in here on your bullshit, Lucien. We have a reservation at seven and can’t be late.”

“Stop playing with me. Just a little taste?”

“No! Get dressed.” I tried not to sulk like a big kid, but she was going to pay for that tonight when we made it back home. Quickly, I hopped in the shower to start getting dressed. Tonight was a YSL cologne night. The fresh and woody scent made Keisha a little handsy. Physical touch was my love language. I didn’t like to be touched unless it was my person, apparently, and Keisha was definitely the one I wanted rubbing on me.

My signature color, black, was taking a backseat tonight, and in its place would be a chocolate brown tailored suit with a black button-down shirt. Gotta match my baby for date night.

The drive into the city was tough with Keisha’s sweet-smelling ass next to me. We could have skipped dinner and gone straight to dessert. I needed her in the worst way.

The playlist we listened to made things worse for my growing erection. Those thick-toned thighs were calling out to me, and I had to reach out to wrap my hands around them. That shimmer shit she wore had me ready to dive in headfirst between them.

The venue was an upscale Cajun seafood restaurant that brought out celebrities and dignitaries. I quickly made my way to open the door for Keisha when the valet took my keys. She never needed another man to open her door when I was around. Another man getting a clear view of those thighs would have sent me into a frenzy.

Guiding her through the dining area, we were greeted with all types of emotions. Glances of jealousy and seduction from the women and gazes of envy and lust from the men. As usual, the stride never changed. Confidence exuded from our unit, but a feeling of uneasiness crept across the back of my neck. The feeling of surveillance nagged at the back of my mind.

Keisha went to take her seat as I reached down to grab a handful of ass and caught her look of surprise and mischief as she pulled her chair closer to the table. I needed her wrapped around me real bad.

"Ah, hell. I left my cardigan in the car. Baby, can you get it for me please? I'm sorry."

"If you weren't so fine, I'd let you freeze," I said with a chuckle. Standing to my feet, I looked down and said, "Order me a whiskey neat."

Towering over her, she looked up with that slight blue tint in her eyes, and my imagination went wild with thoughts of her like this later tonight. Walking back to the front, irked, that uneasiness never lifted. It actually intensified. I stretched my neck in an attempt to shake off the tension inside.

Something wasn't right, and all of my years of military training told me to trust that feeling. I spotted the little cardigan in the passenger seat as the valet pulled my car around. Reaching in to grab it, my heart started pounding. I tipped the valet and then hurried back inside.

Briskly heading back to my table, my foreboding was confirmed. Wilton fucking Cartwright. I took a step back behind the large plant close to the table.

"Keisha, I told you I would be seeing you again. You can't get away from me, baby."

Keisha looked up to see who had approached the table, and the look of astonishment crossed her features. Anger then nervousness followed as she looked around the restaurant. She knew I would be back any minute.

"Wilton, you need to leave. Now is not the time or the place for this. How did you even know I would be here?"

"It's fate, baby. I'm not following you. We just happened to be in the same place at the right time. Don't you think that's a sign?" She crossed her arms and prepared for a rebuttal, but he kept talking, "Why do you have that little shit on? You never dressed like that with me." He looked her up and down, licking his lips. "Anyway! Come to the back with me so we can talk?"

"I'm not going anywhere with you. You need to leave. As you can see, I'm on a date."

He scoffed, "With that big dude I heard about, or are you in your hoe phase and hooked up with another dude? I know how females act after a breakup."

Her head swung around to meet his eyes with a glare that could set him on fire. "Get the fuck on, Wilton."

I had heard enough. Coming from the shadows, I started toward the table. Wilton reached down, grabbed her arm, and yanked her from the seat as she was looking away, sipping her water. Her breath caught when our eyes met.

Moving quickly, my hand struck him in the throat. A gurgling sputter escaped his body as he released Keisha and fell to the floor. His hand shot up to his throat as he struggled to catch his breath. I grabbed Keisha, pulling her into a hug as I kissed her hair.

He was lucky he tried it in a restaurant. The wait staff hurried to his aid on the floor, asking if he needed emergency assistance. When the owner approached, I informed him of the incident and slid him a hundred-dollar bill to quietly dispose of this little issue. I was on a date with my lady, and that bum wasn't going to ruin it. He needed to go somewhere else and die instead of here. The owner apologized for the disturbance and then picked him up from the floor. Wilton finally looked at my scowling face as he was assisted to a standing position. His eyes widened as a crease formed on his massive forehead. His lips spread apart slightly as if... he recognized my face from somewhere. The owner ended Wilson's stupid ass venture down memory lane and carried out the trash.

"Are you ok?" I whispered in her hair. She didn't speak but shook her head, yes. I could tell she was shaken up and pissed. "Let's go. I'll have them send some food to the house." Grabbing her purse and cardigan, I led us out of the building.

As I drove, I hung my right arm over her thighs. "You know I'm going to kill him, right?" She looked into my eyes with earnest concern, then threaded her fingers through mine and kissed the back of my hand.

"Just be careful. I can't lose you," she said solemnly. Sad that it had to come to this. I knew she didn't want him to die, but it was inevitable at this point. He wasn't going to stop, so he had to be stopped.

That was all the permission I needed. I never wanted her to worry about her career, and definitely not her safety. I just needed time between tonight's incident in front of witnesses and the time I decided to strike. Calculated and ruthless was my method.

Grabbing Keisha out of the car, I carried her bridal style inside my home. She was quiet the entire ride home. "I know it has to be done, I just hate that it has come to this. I know he isn't going to stop," she whispered quietly into my ear.

I understood her feelings. This was someone she once loved, was going to marry, and now was destined for death. Slow and painful if I had it my way. She needed to be reminded that her man had her in every way. We walked through my pitch-black home to my bedroom. Placing her on the bed, I bent to sit on the floor and removed her shoes. Staring in her eyes, I kissed the top of her foot.

"You are mine." I kissed her calf.

"I take care of what's mine." I kissed her thigh. Pulling her dress up around her waist.

"I love you, Keisha. I promise to take care of your mind, body, and soul." I pulled her dress over her head and exposed another rose-gold, lace bra and panty set. Watching me with heavy-lidded eyes, she let me have complete control.

"You need to be reminded who you fucking with and how I get down. I'll do what's necessary to protect you." I kissed up her chest, then her neck. She moaned as I licked over her body. Hovering over her body, I held my weight on my elbows, so I didn't crush her. Reaching up, clasping her fingers together behind my head, she brought my lips to hers, then plunged her tongue into my mouth. Her eagerness excited me.

I stepped back from her to undress and watched her finish unwrapping my present. The most gorgeous chocolate nipples stared back at me. Climbing back onto the bed, I lined myself up with her entrance and fell deep inside her love. Bottoming out, I paused for a moment so both of us could adjust.

As I began to move, she wrapped her legs around my waist. "Let me hear you enjoying this shit," I grunted in her ear as my strokes intensified. This wasn't just sex; this was me expressing my love for my woman.

Her cries of ecstasy grew louder as I rocked inside of her. Grabbing her by the waist, I picked her up and changed our positions. I lay on my back and positioned her on top of me. She rode me soft and sweet, and her breast bounced on my face. The faces she made fueled my stamina as I pounded into my baby. Her hair swung wildly as she lost herself. I reached up to grab her by the neck and pulled her ear to me. I intertwined our fingers with my other hand as I spoke in her ear.

"Take your dick. You know it's yours?"

Overwhelmed by the sensation, she couldn't speak. I looked up into her face to see her eyes rolling to the back of her head. She took it all with her mouth, hanging open in an O shape. Her tight pussy massaged my hardness as I continued to caress the ridges of her G-spot. "Shit!" I growled in her ear at the wet goodness surrounding me.

I muffled her cries with my mouth on hers. Her body locked up as her pussy tightened, letting me know she had reached her pinnacle. My strokes became rigid as she milked me to my orgasm, and we came together.

We lay there a few minutes until we caught our breath. The dimmed light in the room hit her naked body just right to have me ready for another round. Walking into my ensuite bathroom, I turned the shower on to the perfect temp for Keisha. Hell.

Bodies washed, sheets changed, we fell asleep in the bed, wrapped up in each other. Our heartbeats synced, and mine content. I was in love with this woman.

An urgent sound called my name.

"Lucien! Lucien! Help me!" The voice familiar, but no one was around. I spun around in an empty warehouse looking for the voice.

"Lisette? Where are you?"

"No, it's me. Help me, baby! We need you."

Chapter 15

Wilton

Who the fuck was that big ass man Keisha was dating now? Shit just got a lot harder with him in the picture. I need to catch her alone so I can talk some sense into her. I wasn't expecting a stealthy, Black Bruce Banner, Incredible Hulk looking-ass to come from around a corner and sneak up on me. That was really the only reason he got me like that. He wouldn't catch me slipping next time though.

Knock, knock! "Sir, the doctor has signed your discharge papers. Here are your orders for recovery. Next time, be more careful. We don't need you slipping in the shower again."

Rolling my eyes, I snatched the paperwork from her hand as she quietly giggled, then turned to walk out of my room. That big motherfucker hit me so hard I thought I was dying. I had to drive myself to the hospital because I couldn't stop the burning in my throat.

Now my neck was covered with this purple-ish bruise, and I could barely speak. I have to figure out how to make him pay for that. He didn't know who I was. My connections stretched for miles. I would get him. Both of them.

Moving slower than normal in these freezing temps, I gathered my things and then headed out of this hospital. The sterile smell of disinfectant and sick people made my stomach turn. Since I could barely speak, I pulled my phone out to send a text to my uncle.

He raised me like his own child since my own father was worthless. Washington Cartwright was just a flunky for my uncle, Otis. Whatever he needed, my dad was there doing his dirty work.

My mom was one of the working girls turned house mom. She would take care of all of the girls who came into her house until we expanded. There were about five houses filled with women and children, my family took, and each one had a different house mom. Often they just promoted a female who didn't have what it took to "work" or was too nurturing to become the house mom. I knew them all now since I was bounced around between all of the houses.

As I walked out of the hospital doors, I paused to take in my surroundings. Checking the parking lot to see if the Incredible Hulk was anywhere around, I walked as quickly as I could to my car.

Me: We have a problem with Keisha. She has a new boyfriend. I can't even talk to her now.

Unc: You don't have a choice nephew. Get it done. By any means necessary. Don't make me have to get involved.

Desperately searching my brain, I came up blank on how to get close enough to convince her that we need to be back together. I'll even let her dress like a slut, like tonight. She never wore stuff like that with me. She was always in pants whenever we went out.

It didn't matter if we were just going to my family's home or going up the road to grab food. She was so bland with her blue jeans or slacks. Ugh! That hair was always a mess—big, wild, and frizzy. Once I have her back under my spell, I could get her dressing the way I like and wearing her hair in a more polished style.

The drive back home was loud with my thoughts. My mind was so consumed with ways I could get her back that I didn't remember the drive here. My family's connections with the local coven could help me obtain wolf's bane.

Keisha forgot I knew her little secret—she was a panther shifter. I would use that little gift to get her to play my game. She would leave Bruce Banner and be with me.

Chapter 16

Keisha

Lucien finally released me from the captivity of his home. After that incident with Wilton's stupid ass, Lucien has been obnoxiously clingy. Although I love him being wrapped around me, I was grateful for the break in my own space.

He started having night terrors again after our date night. I know my baby suffered loss with his sister, and his brain was making him think he would lose me, too. Until he went back to a therapist, all I could do was reassure him that it wouldn't happen. Who would be crazy enough to try to kidnap a panther shifter?

Waking up in my own bed this morning felt foreign. There was no cedar wood smell assaulting my nose, no heavy arms wrapped around my body, no hot breath on my neck. My body felt heavier this morning. A sickness in the pit of my stomach overwhelmed my senses and caused me to gag.

The sun coming from the bedroom window triggered my bladder with an urgent need to be emptied for my morning bathroom run. Swinging my legs out of my queen bed, dizziness washed over me. Nausea raged in my stomach, and projectile vomit flew from my mouth—hot and acidic.

Last night's dinner must have been going bad on my stomach. Vomit was everywhere, my bed, the floor, and all on the front of my night clothes. Groaning, I stood slowly to head to the bathroom for a complete overhaul. I grabbed my cell phone, some more clothes, and then turned the shower on the hottest setting to get some relief.

Standing at my vanity brushing my teeth, my phone lit up with a call from my twin, Aaliyah. Answering on speaker, I said, "Hey!"

"Eww, you sound sick. What's wrong?"

"Girl, I don't know. I must have eaten something bad. I just threw up all on myself." Wetting my face towel, I cleaned all of the residual sleep and toothpaste from my face.

"That ain't it. I bet yo ass is pregnant."

"Hell naw, Aaliyah. Don't say that. I'm in a good place in my career. Now is not the time."

"I get it, I swear I do, but have y'all been doing anything to prevent it?" she asked sheepishly because she knew the truth would piss me off.

I huffed out a deep sigh because she was right. I hated it too. As my brain began to spiral, vomit rose in my chest, causing me to rush to the toilet. Vomit spewed from my body like a demon being cast out. It caused my body temperature to rise and a cold sweat to form on my forehead.

"Uh huh. You need to take your ass to get a pregnancy test. Today!"

"Ugh! I'm going. Let me get myself together. I'll call you when I leave the drug store." Dragging my body back to the vanity, I rebrushed my teeth and gargled with mouthwash, then hopped in the shower to wash my stinking ass.

Throwing on a pair of blue jeans, sunglasses, and a graphic T-shirt was going to be the outfit for today. I barely had the strength to do any more than that. I hadn't eaten, and I was sure my stomach was empty from all of that puke my body expelled. The sunglasses stayed on as I walked to the family planning section of the drugstore to retrieve a pregnancy test.

The store was completely empty as I walked to the cashier to check out, so I leaned in and whispered, "Can I use your restroom to take this?" Gesturing to the test in my hand. She smiled warmly as if she understood the urgency in my situation. Pointing to the sign in the back of the store, I thanked her and then headed there.

Handling my business, then washing my hands, my entire body shook from the anxiety of finding out what was going on with me. Looking at myself in the mirror, my panther's blue eyes stared back at me. I knew the answer without even looking at the test. My panther had been subdued today, and I'm sure there was a reason for it.

The test confirmed what I already knew. Positive! Aaliyah called my phone, but I just let it go to voicemail. I smiled as I walked out of the store, but it wavered as my bottom lip quivered. Wrapping my arms around my waist, I trotted to my car.

Might as well head to get food; there was nothing that could be done now. I passed up Lucky's Wingspot in order to avoid running into anyone I knew. I decided to get wings from another sports bar with an empty parking lot. Lucien turned me on to this place a while ago, so I decided to take my chances.

I found a corner booth to tuck into and rethink life. *What will Lucien think? Oh God, I hope he will be happy with this news. What if he isn't? What if, after his sister, he doesn't want kids?*

Opening my email, I sent a message to my sergeant about taking a leave of absence. I needed to figure this out before I could get back to work. *How could I go back to work? I have never seen a pregnant detective.*

Oh God! Putting my head in my hands, I practiced my breathing to calm my emotions. My panther sensed a presence close to me. I raised my head, my vision blurred from holding my eyes shut with my hands.

"I knew fate wanted us together. I passed by this place and saw your unmistakable cobalt blue car." He stood there with a smirk on his face as he looked down on me.

"Now is not the time, Wilton. I'm not feeling well and just want some time alone." He raised his hands in surrender as I grabbed my glass of water for my dry throat.

"I just want the chance to talk to you without your bodyguard present. We really skfhosh snooshhed." The words he said sounded distorted, and his face looked weird. My body started feeling heavy. I couldn't control my body as I leaned into him.

Why is he picking me up? I tried to scold him, but my words slurred as I talked with my heavy tongue. He cradled me in his arms as he carried me out. Something wasn't right. I could hear him tell the workers that I was his wife and had just gotten sick, so we were leaving. As hard as I tried to fight through it, my body was tired, and my eyes were heavy. Giving in, I rested my head on his chest and let the darkness take me.

Chapter 17

Lucien

Waking up without Keisha was hell. Holding her in my arms at night had me spoiled. I was going to try to give her some space since I had been living in her skin these last few days, since the incident with that jackass.

I guess I should go into the office today to help keep my mind off my baby. That dream I had the night of the incident really messed my head up. Had me rethinking my stance on going back to a therapist. This nightmare had my memory of my sister being snatched distorted into it being Keisha. She was calling out to me for help, and I couldn't find her.

That memory was etched in my brain and caused heart palpitations. If it wasn't for Keisha being there that night, I wouldn't have been able to calm my nerves. I was a man in love, and I couldn't lose her too. As much as I fought against even entertaining a date with her, now I couldn't see my life without her.

I needed to get Má on the line to hear her thoughts on it. After dressing for work and heading to my truck, I dialed my mom's number.

"Hey, baby! I was just about to call you."

"Oh, really! Why, what's up?" I said as I pulled up to a red light.

"Lu, I dreamt of fish last night. You got something to tell me?"

Sitting in my truck, stuck, my breathing stopped at her words. *What? Is Keisha pregnant? When did that happen? Does Keisha already know, and she just hasn't said anything?*

A car horn blaring shook me out of my state of shock. I had forgotten that I was driving into work. "Naw, Má, I don't know anything about that," I said with a shaky breath.

"I understand, baby. She may not know yet. You'd better get to her though. I been dreaming, Lu. Remember what I told you before you started dating. My brain went back to our previous conversation:

She is the one for you, Lu, and you gon' have to be patient with her. She been hurt before, but that's not the end of her pain. Especially if you choose not to be around. She needs you, my baby.

"Yes, Má, I remember."

"Well, find out and call me back. I need to get ready for my grandbabies."

My mom was so excited, and I hadn't even confirmed anything. I needed time to process this news myself. *I might be a daddy? Could I be a good daddy?* Needing to talk to Keisha, I dialed her number, and it rang until the voicemail picked up.

She must be busy and not able to talk, so I sent her a text. Sitting in my truck outside of my office, the nervous energy had me ready to head back home. Dang! I didn't get to tell Má about my dream. This new information had taken over my thoughts.

Working through the day was nonexistent as I sat and waited for a call or text back from Keisha. I called a few more times and was greeted with the voicemail again. Finally, I left work on a mission to get some answers. Nobody was that damn busy that she couldn't at least text me back and say something. The last time this happened, she was hemmed up in an alley fighting for her life.

Decision made. I was headed to find my woman. She was still off from work, so she should be home. Getting to my truck, I took off my suit jacket and tie, unbuttoned a few buttons on my shirt, then drove to her house. There was a mix of anxiety and excitement rolling in my stomach. Stopping outside her house, I didn't see any movement. My instincts were to break in and head inside. I needed to make sure she wasn't lying on the floor, dying. This was the exact reason that I made a secret key to her house. As I walked through her home, nothing looked out of place.

Her bed was messy as if she had just rolled out of it and left. There was a slight stench in the bright room. As I turned to leave out of the bedroom, I noticed a pinkish substance with specks of green. It looked to be vomit on her nightstand. The carpet between her bed and the side of the nightstand had the same substance running down. I touched it, and it hadn't hardened yet. This looked like she tried to clean it, but missed this area.

I couldn't think clearly. *Why wouldn't she call me if she was sick? I knew I shouldn't have let her go back to her house.* Pissed was an understatement. I started seeing spots. Now she was out somewhere sick, and with my baby.

I went into her bathroom to wash my hands and saw it was a mess in there too. With shaking hands, I grabbed her puke-covered clothes and brought them up to my face. They smelled just like her sweet scent. I rested my back on the wall, then slid into a seated position.

Is that what my dream was about? Is Keisha in trouble?

"No, it's me. Help me, baby! We need you."

Trying my breathing exercises, I needed to regulate my mind so that I could find my baby. Reaching into my back pocket, I grabbed my phone to call her number again.

Voicemail. This time it didn't even ring. I logged in to my system to pull Aaliyah's number from my files.

"Hey, is this Aaliyah?"

"Yeah. Who is this?"

"It's Lucien. I'm looking for Keisha. I haven't been able to get her on the phone all day. I'm at her house now, but she isn't here. There is just vomit everywhere."

The other side of the line was quiet. Like she knew something she wasn't ready to divulge.

Hesitantly, she said, "I spoke with her this morning, and she was throwing up pretty bad. I convinced her to go to CVS to see what was going on with her. Maybe she broke down and went to the hospital."

Getting off the phone with the other person she was the closest to, my heart wasn't any more settled than before I called. I needed to get to my office to look up if she had checked herself into any hospitals in the area.

My breaths were coming in quick succession, and my hands were now sweating. I had to remind myself that this was not the same thing that happened to Lisette. No one had taken her. She was just probably sick in the hospital with morning sickness.

My mouth said those words out loud, but my body felt that deep down inside, something else was wrong. She would have called Aaliyah or me to let us know what was going on with her. I ran back to my truck and hopped in to get to my home office.

I sat at my desk hacking files from every hospital within a 50-mile radius. Combing through every name and diagnosis—in case she was listed as a Jane Doe. Nothing.

The office was dark and eerily silent, matching my mood. My body walked on autopilot to the pitch-black bedroom. No TV. No radio. Just lay alone with my thoughts. We haven't gone this long without speaking with each other since we met. As my mind spiraled into past memories, my body succumbed to the sleep I fought.

The warmth of the sun heated my face and yanked me from my sleep. My body jerked up into a sitting position when I reached for my phone. My first thought was to check my phone for any notifications. Nothing. No unknown callers or text messages. Unable to wait any longer, I called the one person better than myself at tracking down someone—Jamilah.

"Jamilah, I need your help!"

"Well, hello to your rude ass, too!" Jamilah was the sassy sister, always with a comeback.

"Have you heard from your sister?"

"Not in a few days, what's up?"

"I haven't told anyone, so keep this quiet. She is missing. I haven't spoken to her. This is day two. That's not like her. We talk every night."

I could hear her breath hitch. "Are you sure she's missing and not just taking a break from your ass?" The hope in her voice told me she was worried as well. It wasn't like Keisha to come up missing, and no one has heard from her.

"Not this time." I tried to keep the sadness out of my tone, but I know I failed miserably.

"I'm going to tell my dad. He can help, too, but in the meantime, I'll get to work tracking down her car. I'll pull all footage from the traffic cams within a 30-mile radius of her home. We will find her."

I knew contacting Jamilah would be a good idea. Pacing the floor, I couldn't wait to hear something. Up, down, up, down, my breathing mimicked my pace. Pumping out a hundred pushups, I needed to burn some of this anxious energy when my phone rang.

My body leaped off the ground to grab my phone off the table. "Tell me something good, Jamilah." I rushed out breathless as I leaned against the wall, waiting for my heart rate to regulate.

"I see she went to CVS, then she left there looking like she had seen a ghost. She went to a sports bar called Mo's. That's where everything goes cold. They have cameras inside, but the system is locked down like Fort Knox. Give me about ten minutes. I'll get into it."

I put her on Mo's when we first met, but her favorite spot was Lucky's Wingspot. *Why would she go there instead?* Deciding not to wait, I grabbed a shirt and laced up my J's, then headed to my truck. Mo's was about to see me, and if Jamilah couldn't hack the system, I would knock some sense into the owner to gain access. If the modern way didn't work, the option to go old skool always got results.

The music in the truck was on silent, but my thoughts were loud. *This had to be punishment. I didn't deserve this love. I hadn't finished my mission of finding my sister, or at least dismantling the ring that started it all in my life.*

Just yesterday, I was excited for a new life when everything was ripped from my grasp. My lady and my baby were gone in the wind. I slowed the truck to a creep as I turned the corner. Mo's wasn't open just yet, so I didn't expect many cars out front. Boom! There it was. That cobalt blue Audi sat out front.

Whatever happened, this was her last stop. My palms sweated as a cold chill ran up my neck. The jarring sound from my truck's speakers brought me back to the present. Jamilah's name showed on the infotainment center. "Hey! I'm sending you a video from the inside. Prepare yourself for this. If you're driving, pull over."

I hung up, confused as hell. She didn't seem too worried, so it couldn't be that bad. I parked my truck in a space right beside Keisha's car. The video caught a great view of Keisha sitting in a booth, looking like she was working some things out on a notepad. She made a few phone calls, then put her head in her hands. Why was she overwhelmed? Wilton walked to her table and stood next to it for a few seconds. He went into his pocket, grabbed a packet of something, and poured a white powdery substance into her drink. *What the hell was that?*

When she raised her head and realized he was there, the disgust was written all over her face. She reached to grab the water. "No, no, baby, don't drink that," I said out loud as if she could hear me. As she drank the water, my stomach dropped. My blood boiled. I didn't know what was in the water, but I knew it wasn't no damn vitamin C. She looked to be about to go off, but her head swayed. She was feeling something weird now. It was written over her face. She started slumping to the side when he caught her in his arms.

I beat the steering wheel as I continued to watch him cradle her to his chest as she went unconscious. All I saw was red, and I needed his blood. He would die! Soon!

Chapter 18

Keisha

With my right eye swollen, stomach growling, and the stench of acid in the air, I was awakened from whatever drugged coma my body was placed in. Soreness riddled my entire frame as I tried to sit up from the floor. Looking around the room, they had me lying on the hard floor of a small room with dirty carpet. The bare white walls and the dirty mattress let me know this was no five-star resort.

My bladder begged to be released from the shackles of this urine. Based on the wet clothes I had on, I'm sure I lost that battle a few times since I had been here. I tried to cover my nose but realized my hands were bound behind my back. Outside of my room door, I heard muffled voices. It sounded like they were arguing.

"What the hell is going on here? Why is her face swollen?" A woman's voice quietly fussed at someone. The other voice sounded like Wilton.

"I know. She kept fighting, even with the medicine to knock her out. I had to do something."

"Otis is going to be pissed when he finds out you brought her here. Then, when he finds out you hit her... You know what? Just leave, I'll take care of her."

Take care of me? What does that mean? Is she going to finish what he started? I needed help, though. I could appeal to her womanhood and get her to get me some clean, dry clothes. Worst-case scenario, I could whoop her ass and try to escape. Trying to stand on my feet, I used the dirty mattress against my shoulder to balance on, then dizziness took over.

I didn't feel my panther and couldn't shift. Shit! I had forgotten I was pregnant. Shifters can't shift into their animal form during pregnancy. The human body could morph and contract, but when there was another human inside, it prevented the shift to keep the baby safe.

The door creaked open, and in walked a deep brown-skinned woman carrying a tray of food. My heart melted at the sight of eggs, bacon, fruit, and bottled water on it. Her eyebrows drew together when we locked eyes. She brought the tray closer to me as her eyes scanned my body.

"Oh, chéri! I'm so sorry. Let's get you into some clean, dry clothes." She set the tray on a night table next to the bed. I sat in shock just staring into her eyes. I wasn't sure if she was sincere, so I kept quiet. With my one good eye, I watched her cross the room. Watched her mannerisms, her body language, and tried to tap into my panther senses as much as possible. I couldn't scent any deception, but it could be the baby already taking over.

She disappeared back out of the door, then returned with a few towels and what looked to be clean clothes. Still silent, still leery, I just sat and watched as she gave me instructions, then pointed to the bathroom. She leaned over me and my body stiffened. My brain worked overtime thinking of my next move. If she was trying to harm me, I couldn't do much without my panther and having my hands tied behind my back. I was released from the ties, then she stepped back with her hands up, letting me know she wasn't a threat.

This woman was a Godsend, whoever she was. My vision was still kind of blurry, only working with one eye, but I saw her spirit shining bright.

"When you are done, I should have some clean sheets on the bed for you to rest." She looked over her shoulder at the door, then started to whisper, "I don't condone what Wilton is doing. He said he was bringing his ex-girlfriend here, but I didn't know it was in this condition. I'll bring you ice for your face when you come out." The mystery woman never gave me her name but turned and walked out of the room, leaving me alone with my thoughts.

What had I gotten myself into? I rubbed my wrist as I tried to stand again. On shaky legs, I struggled to the bathroom. Whatever he drugged me with was still in my system. My system might take longer to rid the poison from my body with the baby. Standing face to face with my reflection, my heart dropped at what stared back at me. My right eye was swollen shut, and blood stained my skin as my lips bulged from my face. Trembling, I started the shower.

The bathroom was bare but clean. Hand soap at the sink and a white plastic shower curtain were the only decor in the small room. After taking my shower and slowly cleaning my face, I went to lie down. I wish there was some sort of shampoo to wash the blood and possibly vomit and urine from my hair. Just as she promised, there were clean sheets and even a pillow waiting for me. I finally ate the breakfast she brought me. Now full, I decided to take a nap. As soon as my head hit the pillow, I was up running to the bathroom to give up all of that breakfast that I had this morning.

Using my face towel, I ran some hot water on it to wipe my face again. Crossing the bathroom threshold into my temporary holding cell, I stopped in my tracks. Wilton sat on the edge of the bed, waiting. His head was down, and he was holding something in his hand as he waited for me to come closer.

"When I brought you here, I just wanted some time alone with you so we could talk." He slowly raised his head and turned to look at me. There was a deranged look in his eyes as his jaw twitched from the grinding of his teeth. He held an intense, cold stare as if he waited for me to respond. Slowly, he raised his hand, and in it was the pissy stick with the positive results clear as day.

His voice low and calm, he said, "You let him get you pregnant?" There was a pause in the air. "Now, I need to get rid of that little bastard because I'm not raising another man's baby."

My face drew up in confusion, but I stood silent. Daddy taught us that people love to talk, and if you give them the space, they will tell you exactly what you want to know and more. Wilton turned his head to the side, not understanding my confusion. He had to know I refused to go back to him by now.

"We will be together, Keisha. You don't have a choice. I've been working on myself." He stood abruptly and then started pacing the floor in front of the bed. "I need this to work. I put in the work that you said you required before we broke up. Now you're still refusing me."

He paced, talked, but he wasn't talking to me. More to himself when he said, "I started going to therapy. The therapist said I was making progress. That's good, right? It should be good, right?" My mind shouted at me to find a way out of this room. He was spiraling, and I didn't want to be at the other end of things when he snapped.

I looked around the room, but there was nothing. No possible weapons, not even an escape route for me to run. His pacing blocked the doorway. Maybe I could distract him. "Wilton!"

I called out suddenly. "Where is the lady who was helping me earlier? She said she would bring me something."

Laughing maniacally, he said, "I sent that bitch away. She was too invested in my business. Can't trust that."

Things just got worse for me. As he paced, I decided to just take my chances. Breathing in deeply, I made the decision to go for it. As he turned to walk toward the door again, I ran around him right out of the room. As I passed another room, there was a kitchen to my left. I ran toward a door that looked to be my way out, and excitement coursed through my body. I was almost there. *Keep going! Almost there.*

A sharp burning pain shot through my scalp as Wilton grabbed my matted, tangled hair and yanked me to the floor. He stood over me as he breathed harder and balled his fists. My face paled as I saw the fury in his eyes. *Shit! Shit! Shit!*

His movements were all a blur as a stinging sensation crossed my already battered and bruised face. The slap caused my head to fall back to the ground as I covered my face with my hand. Tears formed in my eyes at the realization that I was at Wilton's mercy in here. Whatever his twisted and demented mind came up with, I would just have to endure. Why would he do all of this? Just because I wouldn't take him back? This was on another level, even for him.

He didn't want me when he had me, so why now? Just let me be happy with someone else. The hate in his eyes toward me confirmed that he didn't really want me. He wanted the power over me.

"Why would you make me hurt you like that?" He reached down and scooped me in his arms. I balled up as tight as I could to avoid him. Wilton walked me back to my holding cell and dropped me on the bed. "Don't try that stupid shit again, Keisha. Do you want me to tie you up again?"

Pleading with my eyes, I quickly shook my head no. I couldn't be tied up again. That would ruin any chance I had of escaping. He turned and strolled out of the room. My nervous system relaxed at his absence. Sighing, I lay my head on the pillow and closed my eyes. His return caused a hitch in my breath as I sat up on my elbows. He brought me water.

"Relax! I thought that in this state," he gestured toward my stomach, "You could use some water after your little stunt." I just watched with my mouth open. Not trusting. Not blinking. Not breathing.

The door slammed and locked behind him. I quieted my breath to listen to my surroundings. The walls had to be thick, or he was gone. I looked around the room for hidden cameras or alarms, but there was nothing. Finally able to relax, I grabbed the water and looked in the glass. There didn't seem to be anything in it, and it smelled normal. Drinking it, I brainstormed ways to get out of here until my eyelids grew heavy.

Chapter 19

Lucien

Boom! Boom! Boom! “Are you dead in there? Get yo ass up, Shadow. Now is not the time for that.”

I raised my head off the steering wheel, with my eyebrow raised, then looked out of my window to see Jamilah standing there with her hands on her hips. Gathering myself and evening out my breathing, I lay my head on the steering wheel to focus. I lost track of time. Not ready to hear Jamilah’s mouth, I huffed out a heavy sigh.

“What’s up, J?” I asked lazily. I didn’t have the energy to argue with her today. My soul was hurting.

"Have you called my dad? I think he has the right to know his daughter is missing. Plus, he can help find her. You know, the whole shifter thing," she said with heavy sarcasm dripping from her tone. Keisha told them I knew after the night she killed her partner. They took keeping their identity hidden seriously, so everyone was notified when there was an issue that could put them at risk.

"No," I said, running my hand down my face. How do you tell a father you didn't do enough to keep his daughter safe from being kidnapped? *I should have never let her leave.* "I'll go to his house this morning. This is a conversation we need to have face-to-face."

"Good, I'll have Nia and Aaliyah meet us there." She rushed back to her car, fingers flying across her phone screen, as I started my truck, dreading this conversation. Timothy and I had a lot in common, especially the love we both have for Keisha. The drive was shorter than normal. I don't even remember how I got here or stopping at any lights.

Hopping down from my truck, my muscles tensed, my jaw clenched. *Má, Lis is gone! She isn't in the front anymore. There is smoke in the front, and her red sandal is still here. Má! Má! I screamed as I realized she had been taken.*

Lucien! Lucien! Grabbing my shoulder, Timothy snapped me out of my spiraling. My body shook from the memory. The heaviness of his hand grounded me, bringing me back to the moment. I couldn't form the words, looking into his weary eyes, he knew something was wrong.

"Son, tell me what's wrong with my daughter," Timothy stated with wariness written over his face.

As I opened my mouth to explain everything, tires screeching could be heard down the street. Timothy, Jamilah, and I stood and watched as a maroon, two-seater Cadillac peeled into the circular driveway. Xavier drove, but before he could put the car in park, Nia was out, sprinting toward us. Aaliyah's burnt orange Lexus SUV flew in behind them. She jumped out with tears in her eyes as she jogged up to us.

Jamilah said, "Let's go inside guys." The mood was somber as we all walked into the Grants' family home. No one took a seat as we stood around the living room. Timothy went to his bar and made an Old Fashion before we started with the news. The anxiety in the room was at an all-time high as they waited for me to start talking. I paced in front of the couch, trying to get my thoughts together.

Jamilah reached into her back pocket to grab her phone. Jamilah got straight to the point in work mode. Her back straight and voice stern, she said, "I sent everyone the video. This is what we are dealing with." The range of emotions that flashed across everyone's face went from sadness to horror, then to anger as they viewed the video. Nia's hands began to shift as fur sprouted from her wrist. Xavier grabbed her shoulders, then leaned in to calm her as he explained that we needed a plan first. Timothy looked down into my face as I sat on the couch, thinking, and said, "How long has she been missing?"

Jamilah responded, “It’s only been two days, but I just got this video today. I can’t get a location on her cell phone either.”

Standing to my feet, I gathered myself and exhaled a deep breath, then stated, “I’m going to kill Wilton when I get my hands on him.”

Timothy said, “Not if I get my hands on him first!” He shifted into his panther. His eyes gleamed a metallic silver as the muscles flexed through the shiny black coat.

Walking to the door on a mission, I heard bones cracking as Aaliyah, Nia, and Jamilah also shifted. They were all massive, but not as large as Timothy. The eye colors the only noticeable difference between them. There was gold, green, and a reddish pink. The cobalt blue was the missing piece. A pain shot through my chest at the thought.

Xavier yelled out to me, “I’m riding with you!” My eyebrows shot up in surprise at his declaration. I knew he still had some hostility toward me from that ass-whoopin’ my guards put on him at my warehouse. We hopped in my truck, watching the silent display of power and agility as the Grant family ran full speed ahead into the woods toward Wilton’s home.

I didn’t have time to babysit a grown man's feelings, so I ignored Xavier as we sat in silence across town. There were no hard feelings on my end, I was focused on getting my girl back. If Wilton harmed a hair on her head, I would make his ending as drawn out and painful as possible.

Looking forward, quiet, Xavier broke the silence and said, “Look, I understand you did what you thought you had to do to stop trafficking. Now that I know more of the story, I ain't mad at you." I just looked at him with a frown on my face. Truthfully, I didn't give one fuck if he was still mad. My pregnant girlfriend is out here, possibly being harmed.

"This is not a kumbaya moment. I just want you to know, I'm riding with you. Didn't want you to think I wouldn't do what was necessary to help my sister-in-law over some old shit." He reached into his back to pull out his Glock nineteen and checked the magazine.

That made sense, but with or without him, I was running in guns blazing for mine. No other words needed to be spoken, I looked him in the eyes and nodded my understanding. My mind was focused on getting Keisha back and in one piece. This must have been what Má kept trying to warn me about. All of that shit was coming to an end.

Pulling up to his small one-story home, the Grants were already sniffing around. The house was just like the owner, average. Beige and bland. Wilton was as simple as they came. I didn't understand what Keisha ever saw in him.

The front door of the home flew open when Xavier and I jumped out the truck, guns drawn. Wilton came outside in just shorts—no shirt, no shoes. His khaki-colored skin, looking like a naked mole rat, was covered with red scratch marks across his chest and neck. My trigger finger started to itch at the moment I noticed them. Xavier stepped closer to me and said, "Hold on! Let's get Keisha first." I forgot he could interpret body communication like a second language.

"What the hell are you guys doing in front of my home?"

"Some remodeling if you don't tell us where Keisha is," I said, cutting straight to the point. "We saw the video of you carrying her out of the bar. Bring her outside, or we are going inside to get her." Putting my pistol in my back, I walked closer to him. I needed to feel the life leave his body under my bare hands; using my tool wouldn't be as satisfying.

"She isn't here, man." he said, putting his hands in the air. There was a slight tremble he tried to hide by moving them to his pants pocket. "Yes, I ran into her at the little wing spot, but when she got sick, I offered to take her to an emergency room."

As he spoke, the panthers were hard at work, prowling around and through the home. The one with green eyes came out of the home, shook its head as if to say no, then walked back toward the woods. I guess that meant Keisha wasn't in there. The rest of the panthers followed suit.

I wasn't satisfied yet. Running up to Wilton, I jumped in the air for added effect. I needed my weight to come down hard as I wrapped my hands around his throat. His knees buckled under my weight and hold. The veins in his forehead popped out as sweat formed at his temples.

"Bitch ass ni—"

"Shadow!" Xavier yelled as he ran up and grabbed my arms to stop me from choking the life out of Wilton. "We need him alive in case we have to get info from him."

He was right, but I didn't want to hear that shit right now. I squeezed a few more seconds staring into his eyes as tears dropped from them. The distinct smell of urine made me release his ass with the quickness. "Watch ya back. You never know who is lurking in the shadows."

As we turned to walk away, my brain began to run wild about where she could be. "We'll find her man!" Xavier said as we made it back to my truck. We headed back to the Grant family home to see what we could come up with. Jamilah was hard at work typing away on that computer when we walked in.

"We didn't scent her anywhere at the home besides him and his car. Maybe he did take her to the hospital," Nia said as Xavier, and I walked in and sat on the couch.

Running my hand down my face, I blew out a loud breath. "I called all the hospitals within a 50-mile radius. I even checked the records for all Jane Does. She wasn't there." I looked at her sisters as the mental turmoil wreaked havoc on everyone. "She is pregnant, too." The looks on their faces spoke volumes.

The sisters looked at each other as if they knew something I didn't. "What? Did everyone know but me?"

"It's not that. When a shifter gets pregnant, they can't shift in order to protect the baby, Aaliyah said solemnly. I shot up from my seat at the news. "So that means she doesn't have that extra protection available." Worry etched into my shoulders as my brain realized how vulnerable my baby was at this time. Voice tired and raspy, I asked Jamilah to look into any of Wilton's family property in the U.S.

I know he had something to do with her disappearance, and going to his family would be a great cover. Family will uphold you in your dirt because they love you. If we can find a cousin or something with a stash house, that may be our answer.

"Is anyone going to call Mom and let her know something happened to one of her kids?" Nia damn near whispered as she looked around the room. No one spoke up to volunteer either.

Timothy took a sip from his glass of brown liquor and said, "Naw, I think we should keep this amongst us. You all know your mother is a drama queen. She would tear the city down with her bare claws. Let's keep this away from her job as well, until we know more. Everyone is a suspect."

Nodding in agreement, I spoke up, "Her partner was in on the trafficking and was sent to keep an eye on her. I agree anybody is a suspect, but my intuition is telling me Wilton is where we need to hang our focus." No one was going home tonight without answers. We sat up most of the night thinking of ways to find her.

My body shut down from mental exhaustion. The loop of Lis being taken played behind my lids again. She was joined by Keisha this time. As my body thrashed on the couch at Keisha's family home, my body felt heavier. Opening my eyes, Timothy kneeled next to me, watching like a hawk.

"How long have you dealt with those nightmares?" he said as he handed me a bottle of water. There was no judgment, no fear, just understanding.

"Since my sister was taken as a child, then there was the military, now this mess with Keisha."

"PTSD is serious and should be handled accordingly. That's a weighted blanket." He nodded his head to the dark gray cover he placed on me during my night terror. "They help with calming the nervous system, but you should see a therapist as well. That's a major part in taking care of yourself."

I chuckled as I sat up on the couch. "You sound like Keisha. She was always preaching about mental health."

"We're going to find her, son. I see that you really care about her, and now you have another reason to bring them back home safe."

"Yeah, you know I'm tearing whoever has them limb from limb. My heart and my baby." I shook my head as my mind brought up thoughts of them being in danger.

"Get some rest. You can keep the blanket," he said, patting me on the shoulder then walked out of the living room.

Chapter 20

Keisha

The quiet hum of the air conditioner pulled my body back to consciousness as I opened my eyes. Stillness in the building exacerbated my feelings of despair. The sparse room gave the same hollow feeling as last night when my body gave in to whatever that was in that glass of water. With a heaviness in my body, I struggled to keep my eyelids open.

Wilton drugged me, and this was how I was going to die. Why did he hate me so much that he would kidnap and drug me? I should have known leaving him in my past wouldn't be that easy. "Guess I just couldn't be happy." I lay in bed and sulked.

The door to the room creaked open with a tall, slender figure standing in the threshold of the room. With my vision blurred, I couldn't make out the face, but I was certain it was Wilton. My body was heavy, and my lids drooping, I just lay there and accepted my fate. With the pregnancy, my panther was suppressed to keep the baby safe.

"I see the wolfsbane is working as described. I got your feisty ass right where I need you. Maybe now we can talk." He walked over to the bed and sat on the edge as pain shot through my stomach. My face bawled up in a tight scowl, but I immediately corrected. I didn't need him to have any more advantage at this moment.

Wolfsbane? How does he know about that? It's the only thing that could suppress my Panther and make me weak. He must have put a shit ton in the water from last night. That explains why I can't mind linking with my family. They have to know something is going on by now. Wilton doesn't know about mind linking unless he read about it somewhere, but I doubt it. He hated to read.

"What. Do. You. Want?" I forced out with controlled breaths, my body wracked with pain. A dull, throbbing lower back pain settled in as he began talking. The words coming out of his mouth were muffled due to the severe pain my body was experiencing. All I could do was close my eyes and pray that it would end soon.

"Wake your ass up while I'm talking to you!" He screamed out as the back of his hand slammed into my face, causing my cheek to split. Blood trickled down the side of my face as he just looked into my eyes with disdain. "You need to understand that if we have to be together, I'm in charge."

What was he talking about? We didn't have to be together. He could just let me go about my business and live my life. I wanted to be with Lucien. He was probably tearing the city up looking for me by now. My heart hurt with longing for him. Lying there watching the man that I thought I wanted at one time, made me realize that I was in love with Lucien.

His quiet, powerful demeanor allowed me and my panther to rest. I felt safe and cared for with him. Wilton complained about my not dressing up for him as I did for Lucien. Dresses showed up more in my wardrobe because I was allowed to show my inner girly side. Wilton thought he wanted that but couldn't handle what came with it—the protection, the love. Pants became my armor when we were together. A barrier between me and the cold world. I couldn't trust the man he was, to be the man I needed. He couldn't handle business, and so often I was on my own, emotionally and physically.

"My family needs your connections at the department, so we will be together." He said forcefully. "We have to be. I sacrificed too much for this. If you want to keep your family safe, you will be a good little wife." My heart rate spiked at that confession. *What is his family into, to where they need my connections? What did Wilton sacrifice for this? This is so confusing.*

He reached into his pocket and pulled out the old engagement ring he gave me before. The ring that once brought me pride and joy now only invoked feelings of sadness and grief. Reaching under the covers, he jerked my hand out, then shoved it onto my left ring finger. The threat he made to my family echoed loudly in my mind as my heavy body drifted in and out of consciousness.

Hours passed with the paralyzing fear that he would hurt my family or Lucien, on a constant loop playing in my mind. The pain in my back and stomach subsided temporarily, and I was able to crawl to the bathroom. During dinner, I had a decision to make—either continue to be poisoned or starve. I knew he wouldn't stop anytime soon until he killed me or my panther. Too much wolfsbane could have irreversible effects.

The stale air in the room dried my throat as I dragged my aching body to the toilet. A gasp left my mouth when I saw blood soaking my underwear in my pants. The walls started closing in on me. I heaved heavy breaths as my chest constricted. My baby.

The cold, hard floor held my battered and bruised body for hours until a familiar face came in to help me shower. There were no words between us, but she washed my face, gave me clean clothes, and set me back in the bed. When we were done, she was gone.

I still didn't get her name, but she was my angel. How did she get wrapped up with such a monster? According to Wilton, they are all monsters looking to have control over the city. That needed to be stopped. Who had locks on the outside of the bedroom doors, apparently, kidnapping isn't new for them.

Chapter 21

Lucien

The inaudible chatter coming from somewhere on the left side of the room woke me. The sun had not graced the sky with its presence yet, and someone was already up working. My body collapsed on the couch in the Grant family home as we worked tirelessly to find Keisha. I hadn't left since I saw the video.

The constant dreams of Lisette now included Keisha and had my body in a state of stress. I wish I had never let her leave my house. How did I lose two of the most important women in my life? Maybe this was punishment for not successfully completing the first mission I set in place.

My sister was important to me, but I needed a life too. My life didn't end when she was kidnapped. One of us had to live and be happy, but without Keisha, that was going to be hard. I was a child when Lisette was—

"Shadow, I found a few properties with some interesting activity," Jamilah said, interrupting my thoughts. Everyone was using every resource available to them to get tips on the whereabouts of Keisha. Timothy was still trying to keep her abduction under wraps since we didn't know who to trust.

"What you got?" I asked, grunting, as I raised my tired body from the couch. Walking to her make-shift office in the living room, I saw she had a board set up with different properties on a map. There were connections to Wilton, written on sticky notes at each property. Jamilah was one of the best info seekers in the hacking industry.

"This one is really interesting. I had to cross-reference the listed property owner with the business owner. Whoever purchased the property must have known someone might look into them. The property owner is a shell company that is sold every five years to another fake company. Who do you think owns the fake company?" She looked up into my face like I knew what she was getting at. She was giddy about the new information, but I was as lost as a cockroach in a chicken coop. "Ugh! I followed the trail to find that they were all still tied to the Cartwrights."

"Soo, how does that help us find Keisha?"

"Something illegal is definitely going on. I chose this one because the others are still in a Cartwrights' name. Why is this one in a shell company's name? Especially when it's listed as "vacant" and has been for years." She stood up and pointed to the map to further explain that it was in a secluded area and what that could mean. She thought Keisha might not be the only person being kept at that house.

A light bulb went off in my head. I had been looking in the wrong place. It was still pretty early, and everyone was still sleeping in their childhood bedrooms. Jamilah was the only one still up working from last night. "We need to wake everyone up and head over there, J."

"Hold on, big fella. We need a plan. Let's get everybody up before you turn the city red."

She stopped me in my tracks as I headed to my truck. If all of this was true, hopefully, Wilton was enjoying his final hours on this earth. Timothy, Nia, and Aaliyah trickled into the living room for the recap of the findings from Jamilah.

As they talked it out, I paced the floor thinking of my own plan if they didn't move shortly. My woman and my baby could be in harm's way, I didn't care how things looked as long as they were safe and back in my home tonight.

"We need to figure out why he would take her in the first place. This could be an ambush. He knew we would find her. So what was so important that he would risk his life and his family's reputation to kidnap a highly decorated detective of Blackwater Bay?" That was a damn good question, but at this moment, I didn't care about any of that. She needed to be home, safe. They needed to be home, with me.

"Being a detective could be good or bad at this point," Nia said. "She may have information they need or don't want her to have." All eyes turned to me as my brain turned over everything.

The lightbulb went off as I stewed in my anger. "We know somebody was pissed at her for looking into her recent victims. The commissioner had some sketchy activity in his personal life, and she was getting too close to the info."

"What was the sketchy information that she found?" he questioned in an accusatory voice as his left eyebrow raised. He knew something and just needed confirmation.

"He took bribes to use his position to assist some bad people in the abduction and transportation of women and children." My tone turned aggressive as I relived my feelings when I read that file. "Some handsome vigilante handled it and gave the police the info they needed." Every eye in the house rolled at my admission. Timothy chuckled and shook his head. Aaliyah gasped and said, "Could this mean Wilton and his family are in on that, too? They are a part of the trafficking?" My jaw tightened as I thought about that new revelation.

He was going to hurt Keisha if he found out she really didn't have as much info as they thought. We needed to move. "Jamilah, I need that address. I can't sit around and wait for him and his family to hurt or kill Keisha and my baby."

"Sending it now. Shadow!" She stopped typing to look at me. My body stilled, but my mind raced on. "Be careful and bring my sister back. I'll stay here to work things out on this end. If she isn't there we're running into every house on this roster."

Walking to the door, I felt my phone vibrate with the address I needed.

The rest of Keisha's family headed to the back door as they shifted into their panthers. Xavier didn't speak, he grabbed his guns and jogged to my truck. The Grants had become like family. The acceptance—even knowing about Shadow, spoke volumes about the type of people they were.

Timothy connected with me about my PTSD without judgment but concern for me and understanding. I didn't know if he also suffered from PTSD, but it was nice to know there was someone else in my corner besides my mom and Keisha.

These last few months with Keisha had been amazing. She took care of me and my mental health. The connection we had was unlike anything I had experienced before, and I'll be damned if I let someone take that from me.

Hopping in my truck, we sped to the address Jamilah provided. Based on the map she showed me, I decided to park my truck about a mile out so no one would hear us coming. Xavier and I jumped out and sprinted the rest of the way through the woods.

As we jumped over branches, ran around other obstacles, I heard light pattering in the distance. Three panthers were racing toward the same destination. All power, will, and determination were in their stride to get to Keisha.

My phone vibrated in my pocket as we approached the ordinary one-story home. I slowed my paced and since it would not stop buzzing, I grabbed it out of my pants. "Yeah!" I said roughly.

"Keisha is in there, they can scent her from outside. There are several other people in the home, too. Aaliyah sent me a mind link to contact you. They may be innocent, so don't light the place up just yet." She paused for a moment, then said, "Shadow. They can smell blood."

My heart stopped at the sound of all of this information. Who did the blood belong to? Xavier noticed I answered a call and jogged to me. He nodded his head in an attempt to get more info. "It's Jamilah. They say she is in the home with a lot of other people, but they smell blood." My voice cracked as I passed the information along.

"Hey!" he said and snapped my attention back to him from the spiral my mind was already on, "With it being several people in the home, it could belong to anyone. She is going to be ok. We are here now. Let's get in and get her." He smacked my chest as he jogged toward the home and hid behind a bush.

Ending the call with Jamilah, I worked to get my mind right for what was waiting for me behind those walls. Feeling my lungs with fresh air, I jogged up to the nearest bush and assessed the scene further.

The home seemed quiet on the outside. The curtains were drawn shut, and the home had no decorations, no character. The place was quiet. Too quiet. As if the occupants were locked inside with no options to leave.

The dirt-colored front door showed three deadbolt locks. The bland brick home had minimal windows, which lessened our chances of entry. Xavier leaned in and whispered, "There are no cameras. Do you see an entry point?"

I shook my head no as I continued to assess the area. The panther with the silver eyes approached us, my guess is that it was Timothy. He nudged me and then turned his head to walk to the back of the home. We immediately followed quietly to a weak point he pointed out. The back door wasn't as secure. Whoever planned the security missed this, and I was thankful.

Using his leg, Xavier kicked the lock once, twice, then turned the knob. Guns drawn, we carefully swept the home. It was as quiet inside as it was outside the home. Inside, there were cameras in the hall, so we had to move quickly before anyone showed up. The panthers moved around us and passed several locked doors.

Thorough, slow, and methodical, we swept the home. Xavier kicked a door open and gasped at the sight before him. Women clutching children, about ten in one room, crying and scared. What was going on here? He took care of that room, getting them out while we kept looking.

The panther leading the way stopped at a door further down the hall and sat on its haunches. I approached the door slowly, breathing labored. There was a lock on the outside of the flimsy door. I rested my ear to listen for anything moving on the other side as I decided to use my shoulder to break the door down.

The door split in half as my body stumbled on the other side into the small room. There she was, passed out in the bed. Her body splayed out, limp on the bloodied mattress. The strength in my body left me at that moment as I crashed to my knees at the threshold of the room.

Timothy's panther jumped over me to go assess Keisha. She was non-responsive as he nudged her lifeless body. Tears formed as anger radiated through my body. My phone buzzed again. Knowing it was Jamilah, I pulled it out of my pocket and held it silently. Not knowing what would have left my body if I tried to speak, I just held it to my ear.

"Shadow! Get your ass up. She isn't dead. My dad says she has been poisoned. He can smell the wolfsbane on her breath." I didn't know what the hell wolfsbane was, but it sounded better than death. I'll take it. Lifting my head, a renewed sense of energy swept through me. "Grab her and bring her here."

Cradling my baby in my arms, I walked out with a mix of emotions. We walked to the front of the home to see over a dozen women and children outside. Jogging up to me, Xavier said, "These women were locked in other rooms of the house. I called in an anonymous tip to Blackwater PD. They should be here shortly. We need to get out of here if we don't want to stay for questioning."

Overwhelm clouded my mind with the number of women and children abducted. These sick bastards must have been using this as a holding house until they could ship them out. I recognized a few faces from recent news segments. I informed them all that we had alerted the authorities, and they should be here soon before Xavier, Keisha, and I headed back to my truck.

Nia shifted to her human form before we came outside. She told Xavier that she and Aaliyah would stay around the ladies in the shadows in their panther form to make sure nothing happened. They would be at the house as soon as the cops arrived. That was great news because I didn't want to wait another minute to get Keisha back to the Grants' home.

Xavier drove my truck back as I refused to separate from Keisha. My heart beat out of my chest as time seemed to stop during the ride. With shallowed breathing, she lay motionless with a pained scowl on her face. My eyes were drawn to her like a moth to a flame, while I studied every feature on her face.

Looking closely, a blue undertone sat beneath her puffy eye. That was more than swelling from tears, this was the aftermath of a physical blow to the face. My body temperature rose several degrees thinking about the havoc to come once she was back to normal.

I stroked her hair as my mind spiraled into a place of darkness and revenge. Her eyelids fluttered before they popped open. With eyebrows drawn together, her body tensed, she looked around the truck and gasped.

Chapter 22

Keisha

Sucking in a deep breath, I looked around the vehicle. Where was I being taken? Who is this? "Get off me. Get off me!" I tried to fight my way out of his hold, but he was too strong for my tired body.

"I got you, baby. It's me. Keisha! Keisha, it's me, Lucien!" he said as he leaned in closer to my ear to calm my flailing body. His scent was everything I remembered. What I missed. What I thought I would never smell again.

My body was too weak and hurt like hell, but I was grateful for his embrace. Lucien lay his head in the crook of my neck as I cried. For my rescue. For my baby. In that moment, I knew.

Slowly losing the fight, my body surrendered to the drugs that were still in my system. Waking in another place felt foreign but familiar all at once. Wires clung to my body as I heard machines beeping in the distance. The first thing my eyes saw was a tall, sexy man in the corner watching me as he spoke to what looked to be a doctor.

The familiar pictures on the wall caught my eye as I took in the room. The comforter was the same one in my old room at my parents' house. "Hel-Hello!" Lucien rushed to my side with a bottle of water. I used the little strength left in my body to sit up. Smiling at Lucien, my cheeks burned at my next move, but it had to be done.

"How is my baby?" I said to the doctor, then looked over to Lucien to see his expression. His face was hard to read as he looked intently at the doctor and waited for an answer. *Did he already know? How?*

Mr. Davis, a wolf shifter, was the supernatural doctor we all used since outsiders weren't privy to our existence. He offered a slight smile that didn't reach his eyes, then walked closer to the bed. "I'm sorry the baby didn't survive. With all of the wolfsbane that flooded your system, there was no chance of the fetus surviving. I'm so sorry for your loss. Get some rest so your body can continue to recover."

He patted Lucien on the shoulder, then turned to walk out. Lucien leaned down to grab me in a hug as I sat numb in his arms. At first, I was devastated about this pregnancy, and now I'm angry. Angry at what Wilton took from me. What he took from Lucien.

My body shook as I continued to sob in Lucien's sweet embrace. My fists clenched around his shirt as his silent strength gave me what I needed in the moment. The quiet relief of being free from Wilton's captivity was abruptly interrupted as my panther emerged. The poison had finally been expelled by the IV's enough for my panther to no longer be suppressed. She was angry. My panther wanted blood. His blood.

Grabbing my shoulders, Lucien looked down into my face and said, "I already know who it was, but I need confirmation. Was it Wilton?"

With tight eyes, I shook my head yes, all while devising a plan. "The doctors want you to stay here one more day, then we get to go home. Move in with me, Keisha. I can't take being away from you after this."

My chest tightened. That was a huge move. Was I ready? Was he ready? This could be grief talking. "I know it seems crazy, but I almost went crazy when you were gone. Baby, I need you with me."

"Are you sure? We can take our time..." He shook his head while I tried to run down the list of reasons why we shouldn't jump into this.

"I love you, Keisha. I want us to be a family when the time is right for us to try again. All under one roof. Under my protection. I failed you the last time, but I won't let that happen again."

"Baby, you didn't fail me." I pulled his face down right in front of mine and looked into his eyes. "Someone exploited a weakness he knew about me. That says more about him than you." Kissing those big lips that I missed so much, I said, "I realized I love you so much during that unfortunate time. All I wanted to do was be with you. If you are serious, then let's do it."

He aggressively kissed me until I pulled away. "We not doing nothing in your dad's house. So get your mind out the gutter." I cackled so loud my dad came to check on us.

He stood tall in the doorway with his arms crossed over his chest. "Good to see you up. Hope you know what all of this means." Staring intently into my eyes, I knew exactly what that meant. "He is a dead man. I want his entire bloodline wiped out."

My breath hitched at his words. I knew my daddy loved me, but I had never seen him ride this hard for me. Things were always business as usual with him. "Don't act so surprised. He tried to take one of the best things that ever happened to me away from us. I couldn't live with myself if I allowed him to continue to breathe the same air we breathe. I realized we don't spend enough time together like I do with everyone else.

I allowed you your space due to your work responsibilities, but that changes after this."

I sat there silenced. All those times I felt my dad loved me, but not like everyone else. I was just good enough to help him with the Onyx Hunt, but not good enough to have a real relationship with. I was wrong, and I have never been happier to be wrong.

Lucien stood by my bed with a smug look on his face. I knew that only meant my dad might have to fight Shadow for first dibs on Wilton. While they figured it out, I snuggled into the covers and let sleep take me so that my Panther and I could finish the recovery process. Things were about to get busy soon, and I didn't plan to miss any of the action.

Chapter 23

Lucien

"Just put everything in the guest room. When we get back, I'll sort everything out. I just need my living room and bedroom clear for us tonight," I said to the moving company while I moved through Timothy's house.

Everyone was still camping out here until the doctor gave us the green light for Keisha. Her body needed lots of rest and IV fluids to push out the rest of the poison that killed my baby and almost killed my lady. Timothy told me the poison was made to suppress her panther so that Wilton could do whatever he needed to do.

The doctor looked for signs of sexual abuse but found nothing. That was good because I didn't want to leave her just yet, but I didn't know if I could have held it together if they had found anything like that.

I struggled to keep my temper in check already about the bruises on her face, but my time with him will come. Stewing in my anger was interrupted by feet shuffling behind me. Nia and Aaliyah were helping Keisha into the living room. She begged them to take her out of that bed. Keisha's spirit was still high, her body just hadn't fully caught up.

"Look at you!" Jamilah said as she stood from her makeshift workstation. "I'm glad to see you up and moving around. It felt crazy watching my busybody sister just lie in bed and sleep all day."

"I'm not back to being a busybody just yet, but I feel much better than I did."

"Yeah, I'm going to need a few more weeks of you at the house before I'm releasing you back into the wild," I said jokingly. "J, what you got there?" I pointed to the hand that I noticed had a printed photocopy of a picture.

"Oh, I was playing around with the info you gave me about your sister. I ran her childhood photo in my facial analysis, then did an age progression of what she might look like today. That could help us identify her if we were to run across her in the future," Jamilah said.

My hands shook as I held it out to take the photo. She was beautiful. Heat encompassed my body as I stared longingly at the picture. Those old feelings of failure crept up in my mind. I needed to get back to the original mission of dismantling everything dealing with abducting women and children.

Keisha sat on the couch, looking up at me, spiraling in my feelings for my sister. "Let me see, babe!" I walked around the couch, dropped next to her, then handed her the picture. A loud gasp brought everyone's attention to Keisha. Her hand flew to her mouth as tears formed in her eyes.

"Baby, what's wrong? Are you in pain?" I said, looking over her body in sheer panic. She pointed to the picture repeatedly as her mouth hung open. "What? Talk to me." Aaliyah came over to kneel in front of her sister to help figure out the issue.

"She...she was at the house." Ice ran through my veins as my body went flaccid into the couch. "She helped me. Came in, helped me shower, brought me food, then left. It pissed Wilton off that she was helping me, so he told her to stay away."

She brought her shaking hand up to her mouth, then her body went stiff. "Wait, she snuck back in me before you all came to get me. She told me his family would be upset to know he brought me there. I think she worked for his family as like a house mom."

"Nia, was this woman at the house that day?" I grabbed the photo and urgently handed it to Nia. While examining it, her face scrunched up as she tried to recall that day, but shook her head no.

"Baby, are you sure this is the woman you saw at the house?"

"Yes, one hundred percent sure. Now that I think about it, she had a slight accent like you get when you're mad about something," she said, confirming my suspicions.

"Jamilah, can you pull up that list of homes you had connected to the Cartwrights again. I'm running into each and every one of them, TODAY!" I commanded with a little more bass than usual in my voice.

I waited over twenty years to find my sister. I'd be damned if I was going to squander this opportunity to get her back. The sheer determination showed on my face as I suited up to head out to the first house.

"Wait, I'm not letting you tackle this alone. If nobody else in here knows how serious you are about getting your sister back, I do." Xavier joked as he walked over to Nia, placing his pistol in his back, then leaned down to kiss her.

She stood as well, then started prepping to go with us. Jamilah grabbed her rifle case from her room and looked at us, "What? I want in on the action, too? Do y'all know what I went through about his sister? I'm going too."

Everyone had jokes about this crazy journey of finding my sister, and I couldn't be happier to have her within my grasp. Keisha was staying at the house with Aaliyah and could catch Timothy up on everything when he got back from his run. I walked to her, sitting pretty on the couch, grabbed the back of her head, and kissed her lips. My forehead lay on hers, as I fought hard to contain my excitement.

"Wait a damn minute!" Jamilah yelled out. My head snapped in her direction. "These properties are connected to an Otis Cartwright. Keisha isn't that —"

"The Police Chief for Blackwater," she interrupted. "What else did you find about him? It looks like they wanted to use me for my connections to both the streets and in the department. Wilton told me his family needed me, so I guess to help them continue trafficking women and children."

"I don't know why I didn't see this before, but looking more into Otis, he lived in Chalmette, Louisiana. The earliest activity I see there was in 1999, then his job transferred him here in 2003."

"That bitch lived only a town away from us in Louisiana. Lisette was snatched in 2003. He must have moved his stash houses here when he came."

Before we headed out to the first house, Keisha called a friend at the Federal Bureau with an anonymous tip about the houses and told them to follow up on the rescued girls from earlier. He was getting a few units ready to meet us at the first house. She told him we had more information but would only give it up after we left them. I needed to get my sister first and wouldn't allow them to get in the way. We had to bypass Blackwater PD, who knows how deep the corruption went.

We drove to house one on Jamilah's list and found a group of women locked in rooms. The home was reminiscent of the one where Keisha was held. Multiple deadbolt locks on the front door and locks on the outside of the bedroom doors. The home was too clean. Sterile.

House two was about five miles from the first home and, oddly enough, blended in with the neighborhood. *Why would they put a stash house in the middle of a neighborhood if they were trying to keep it hidden?* We parked on the next street over and split up. Xavier and Nia walked around the front while Jamilah and I decided to run in through the back door. Using her panther senses, she smelled multiple people in the home.

It looked different. Actually lived in. Decor, curtains, and there were visitors. "Lisette, you were only supposed to go to the grocery store. No one told you to go to the woodland home." The sound of someone involved in a heated argument could be heard outside the back door. My blood boiled at the sound of her name. She was held hostage all these years and kept as their personal servant. Lisette decided to help Keisha, but at what cost?

"I don't know how those people got out, but I didn't do anything wrong, Mr. Otis. Wilton is lying. He brought that woman there, beaten and bloody. I knew you wouldn't want that for her, so I helped clean her up and gave her food. That's it! He was going to let her starve."

"She is right, Wilton. I asked you to convince her, not to kidnap and beat her. What were you thinking? She is a fucking detective. Did you even use your brain? Now we have to kill her and find another way to keep an eye on the streets, but you are not off the hook. Her informant Brian is still out there. I heard he is gay. Now, so are you. Since you royally fucked this up, you have been promoted. Get on his good side."

"Unc, I'm not gay."

"You are now. I'll handle the bitch. Thanks, Lisette, but mind your business from now on."

I couldn't believe what we were hearing. Jamilah stood beside me, shocked and disgusted. I had heard enough and was ready to end this pimping factory. They would all die before anyone got to Keisha again. Giving Jamilah a nod, I kicked the back door in. The shock and fear on everyone's face was perfect. Jamilah attacked the Police Chief, Otis, knocking him out. We needed him alive when the FBI raided this place.

I stood face to face with Wilton, when a mischievous grin spread across my face. This was the moment I had been waiting for since we met. He stalked, beat, and kidnapped Keisha, and I was going to enjoy kicking his ass. The look in his eyes told me he knew what was about to happen. He turned and broke out in a sprint. I roared in laughter as I chased behind him. Most predators enjoyed a good hunt before attacking the prey, and this case was no different.

Wilton had long legs, so he covered more ground faster. He ran out the back door, and I kicked it into gear. Jumping on his back, I caught him right before he made a jump over the fence. This was perfect. I wrapped my big arm around his neck from behind and let my bicep curl, cutting off his oxygen. I laughed maniacally in his ear as life seeped from his body.

When his body went limp, I stood and dragged him back inside. I dropped his lifeless body next to his bitch ass uncle. When he woke up, he would see the consequences of his decisions. A lifetime of fucked up decisions finally caught up to the entire Cartwright family. They would all be in jail before sunset with the info Jamilah dug up. Once we deliver it to Keisha's FBI friend, we could sleep good tonight.

Jamilah mind linked Keisha and let her know the FBI could come get the hostages and take the trash. Nia and Xavier helped the hostages out of the home to the front yard. While I stood in front of the greatest achievement to date. She stood quietly, confused and shaking. With her head tilted to the right, "L-Lu? H-how did you find me?"

My heart slammed hard in my chest as I walked closer to her. "Can I hug you? I never stopped looking for you, Lis." She nodded and took a step closer. Engulfing her shaking body in my arms, my body temperature rose as words evaded me.

Lisette took a step back, looking into my eyes, her skin flushed, before she said, "I-I didn't have anything to do with—"

"We know, Lis. You are a victim as well. The lady that you helped at that house is my girlfriend." Her eyes bulged before a smile spread across her face. "She is very grateful for your help. Keisha is the one who told me you were with them. I'll explain it all later."

Taking a moment to think of how to ask. She had been through so much in her life. Would she want to go back home? Would she want to be alone? I just got her back and wasn't ready to let her go, "Come live with me?" I rushed out. We lost so much time, and I wanted to help her in any way that I could to get her life back on track.

"I don't want to impose on you, Lu. I don't know what to do," Lisette said.

"Say you'll come live with me. I have missed you all of these years. You can come and go as you want or move out when you are ready. This won't be a hostage situation. I just want to take care of you." I was practically begging at this point.

"Ok, Lu. I'll move in with you." Her eyes welled up with tears as she stared at me. "I never stopped thinking about you. I knew you would be something when we grew up. Turns out you grew up to be Hulk," she said as we both chuckled.

We stepped out the front of the home to be met with cameras and news crews waiting to ask questions. I gave a quick interview, then moved on. Keisha's contact allowed us to leave without having to stay and sit through all of the questioning today. He was coming to the house tomorrow to get them out of the way. Knowing a little of the history, he extended some grace to us. Even with the Wilton issue, he cooked up a story that covered my ass.

Chapter 24

Keisha

Waking up to the warmth of the sun in my childhood bedroom and Lucien by my side. My heart smiled at everything that transpired in the last twenty-four hours. Lucien rescued his sister from that life with those tyrants. Wilton was no longer an issue, and the largest trafficking ring in South Florida has been successfully dismantled. My baby had been working at this for years, and I was glad that chapter of his life had closed.

Everyone stayed at my dad's house last night for the last time. We finally broke the news to my overly dramatic mom, and she came and did what she did best. Fussed. She fussed over me. She even fussed over Lisette. She said she had to be her mom for the night. Shirley Grant was pissed at everyone involved with keeping this a secret, but she reveled in all of her kids being under one roof again. She and my dad were still working on reconciling after her big betrayal, but I think keeping this from her put them on even grounds now.

I woke Lucien up so he could start packing all of our things for the next chapter in our story. Like the big ass kid that he was, he ran to wake Lisette up in the guest room. Both of us were moving in with him today, and I couldn't be happier. The adjustments would be great, but my baby was worth it.

Aaliyah decided to hang with us today to help us get in and get what we needed. My body had fully recovered, but she still wanted to be cautious. I hadn't had my first shift yet since all of the wolfsbane, and she feared it would be painful. Now that Lisette was moving in, I had to move a little differently since she didn't know about this side of life yet.

I rode with Aaliyah to Lucien's house to give him and his sister some time alone to catch up. The ride there was kind of quiet as I noticed Aaliyah in a somber mood. "What's going on, sis? You seem different this morning."

"Just thinking about everything. Unlike Lisette, your stay was very temporary, and I'm happy to have you back. You are blessed to have such a good man, sis. He loves you down. I wish nothing but happiness for you two." Her words felt genuine, but so did her sadness. It's been a long road for my twin, dealing with lying men who turned out to be energy leeches. They used her to get where they wanted in life, then moved on with who they actually wanted.

"Today is a good day, Aaliyah. New day, new start. Let the old things fade away while we live life with expectancy in our hearts." I reached out to grab the hand she rested on the armrest and gave it a squeeze. I smiled as she forced a smile that didn't reach her eyes. "We celebrating today, so perk up. I need to get to the store so I can cook tonight."

She whipped her head around to me, then gave me a side eye. "Just because you were poisoned doesn't mean you need to take it out on us. I can go my whole life not knowing what that feels like." She cackled loudly as we pulled into the driveway of Lucien's home.

"Ha ha! I can cook. I may just be a little rusty. You know, with everything I just went through." I put my head down and laughed. The running joke was that I couldn't cook, but I never had to. Mom would always cook, and then when I moved out, she would still bring me food. Now I wasn't Gordon Ramsay, but I could do enough to stay alive.

We walked into his home stuffed full of all of my things. Lucien wasn't playing when he said he needed me here with him. Moving my essentials to the main room, Aaliyah and I worked tirelessly moving things from his guest room. A ringing from my cell phone snapped me out of my concentration. It was Malcolm, my FBI friend, calling for more answers about all of these new discoveries.

"Lucien, Malcolm will be here in about thirty minutes to talk more about everything that happened. Just want to let you know so you don't flip out when a man comes to the door."

He nodded his head, then said, "I'm so glad you know me." Walking out of Lisette's new room, I chuckled as I shook my head. That man was crazy in all the ways I loved. We fixed the living room up just in time for Malcolm to ring the doorbell.

Lucien walked to the door with his hulking form and yanked the door open. On the other side was my friend from the Police Academy, Malcolm Shore. Walking in behind Lucien, my eyes lit up when I saw my friend. We didn't keep in touch as well as we should have, but we could always count on each other when needed. "Hey, Malcolm! Come in. How have you been?"

"From what I hear, better than you," he said as he stepped in to the house. He shook Lucien's hand and introduced himself before he walked behind me to the living room. He was introduced to everyone as we took our seats. Aaliyah sat on the love seat with Lisette while Malcolm and I sat on the couch in front of the television. Lucien, being who he was, decided to lean against a wall and watch everything. Malcolm looked over at Aaliyah and paused for a second, then said, "So tell me what happened."

After going down the long list of events with Lisette, I told him about how my life had been turned upside down. "Once I identified Lisette from an age progression photo my sister created, Lucien was ready to turn everything on its head."

Malcolm recorded everything as we spoke about our experience with the Cartwrights. He couldn't keep his eyes off Aaliyah as we spoke. He leaned forward and turned off the recorder, then said, "So Shadow came in to save the day?" he asked so calmly as he looked at Lucien intensely. My body tensed at his words.

"No, I said Lucien," I said, trying to redirect the conversation. Malcolm never took his eyes off Lucien when he chuckled.

"Shadow, you are a hard man to find. I guess the rumors were true. Once you left the military, all traces of you disappeared." Lucien continued to lean on the wall with his arms folded, not budging. "The FBI has been looking for you for a long time."

My heart pounded in my chest. I trusted this man. I let him into our home only for him to betray me. "Malcolm!"

"It's ok, Keisha. I'm not here to cause any trouble. This is more of a warning. The FBI is looking for Shadow, and he needs to stay in the shadows. I love you like a sister, so I'll do what I can to help."

Lucien still had not budged. He didn't confirm or deny his identity as Shadow either. He just continued to watch Malcolm. "So what's next? Will someone be reaching out?" He finally asked, but his posture didn't change.

"I'm the lead investigator for this case. With it involving a high-ranking official, that is where our focus will be unless we need Lisette to testify. With the info Jamilah sent to me, we may not need her testimony. However, I do have a friend coming into town undercover. He is CIA, maybe you two can go to lunch so—"

"The fuck if they will. He can call her if he needs anything," Lucien shouted, interrupting Malcolm. Malcom laid his head back and roared in laughter.

"Aye, man, I get it! You just got your lady back. I don't want any trouble. I've seen how you get active, " he said, laughing with both his hands raised in the air. "The connect would be good to have. Just think about it, and when you feel more comfortable, reach out." He stood to his feet, letting us know he was leaving, giving one final look to Aaliyah, and nodded.

I walked him to the door as Lucien continued to stand quietly against the wall. He watched our every step as we made it to the door. "His name is Dr. Adonis Rane," he whispered as he handed me a card. I leaned in to hug my friend and thanked him for having my back like always before he left.

Walking back to the living room, Aaliyah turned on the television as breaking news flashed across the screen. Apparently, the FBI had seized millions of dollars worth of contraband and police equipment and released hundreds of women and children from captivity. This operation spanned across ten properties, all connected to Blackwater Bay Police Chief, Otis Cartwright, and his family. The brief interview that Lucien did with the local news station, coming out of one of the homes, was being aired.

Lucien's phone rang right after that segment. "Hey, Ms. Sharon! Yes, I just saw it. Please reach out to Malcolm Shore and provide them with the accommodations for the women. This is why we built Lis House. I'll send you his contact info. Thank you! Bye!"

He asked for Malcolm's number to text Ms. Sharon. "Ok, ladies! We need to go to the grocery store. Would you like to go with us, Lisette?" As we made plans to hit a few stores, Lucien's phone rang out loud, which was unusual. That phone stayed on silent. I didn't even know it could ring. He answered it on speaker without even looking at the caller ID as he continued to text Ms. Sharon.

A sultry female voice rang out in the speakers. "Hey, baby! I just saw your fine ass on the news. It's been too long, I need to see you." The house turned silent as I whipped my head around so fast I damned near hurt my neck. He never picked his head up, but his eyes raised and met my squinted gaze.

"Dee! I'm not coming to see you. What do you want? You know what? I don't give a damn what you want. Stop calling my damn phone. I'm married, and my wife would kick your ass, so save yourself some recovery time." He hung up the phone without even letting her respond. I rolled my eyes and turned back around to finish my conversation with the girls. I'm glad he knew the danger he was in at that moment.

Epilogue

Lucien

Silence. Finally. No night terrors. No unrestful sleep filled with distorted visions. Night was filled with quiet slumber, and mornings were now suffused with sounds of Keisha's moans as I slid inside of her. Her warm, velvety insides were home and peace for me. The slippery feel of her body wrapped around me felt like my little piece of heaven right here on earth. After living through hell, this was all I needed.

Deep stroking her from behind, my chest met her back as I grabbed her neck and brought her face to mine. She moaned in my mouth as I picked up the pace. Her body stiffened as I continued to pound into her from behind. My body followed right behind her as she expelled all of her juices around me. "I love you, baby!" I said as my heart rate came down to a normal rhythm.

Keisha lay breathing hard with her hair splayed across the pillows, wild and free. Just like I loved it. I stood, stretching, to get a warm, wet towel to clean us up while she fell back to sleep. Keisha went back to work a few days ago and almost losing her reminded me to love out loud.

Therapy was teaching me to continue to love those around me and let people in to love me back. The night terrors were few and far between, but when they did come, my angel was there guiding me back to reality. Walking through the bedroom that was once decorated in all black and white, now had more character and color. Every part of my life had been updated by the wild-haired woman who had my heart.

I cleaned my woman then kissed her forehead as I pulled on some shorts to make us breakfast. Keisha and my therapist tag-teamed me to loosen my grip on Lisette as well. She was grown and deserved to venture out into the world a little more.

We all went to visit our mother back in Bayou Grise, Louisiana, right after everything came to a head. She cried like the biggest baby and thanked the heavens for bringing Lisette back to her. Keisha and I planned to leave Lisette there, but she informed us that she wanted to build her new life in Blackwater. Now, with all of her kids living here, Má promised to come out and visit.

The relationship between Má and Keisha always made my heart smile. Their late-night conversations or conspiring, kept me on my toes. Pulling out the eggs and bacon, I moved around the kitchen quietly to get something started for Keisha before she went in to work.

"Hey, baby!" Keisha walked in and leaned up to plant those soft kisses on my lips. "Why are you up so early cooking? Did you forget I took the day off?" She lifted her eyebrow as she hopped on the quartz countertop.

"I did actually. What do you have planned today?"

"Lis and I are going shopping. She and Jamilah wanted to go to the bar tonight, and she feels like she doesn't have the right clothes for that. Then we are going to hit the grocery store so she can cook tonight."

"My sister is not going out with Jamilah's crazy ass," I said, seriously, shaking my head. "They need supervision. I can clear my schedule, what time they going?"

"Sir, you will be here with me tonight. I got a few...ideas of what we can do tonight?"

"Bribing me with booty?" I accused, feigning offense while clutching my imaginary pearls. "I'll allow it," I said as I walked between her legs, sticking my tongue down her throat. Prepping her body for round two of this morning's activity.

Keisha

Finally, being let up for air, I dressed to head out with my future sister-in-law to hit the stores and spend some of Lucien's money. My phone buzzed on the nightstand as I grabbed my pistol and placed it in my back. “Hey, girly! What’s up?” I said to Aaliyah as I answered.

“I needed a break from work, so I took off. I’m tagging along with y’all today. I’ll be at your house shortly so I can ride with you.” Aaliyah had avoided going out since I came home. She was finally allowing herself time to enjoy herself.

After ending the call, I walked in to get Lisette so we could head out. Our relationship had progressed so much since we rescued her from the Cartwrights. She was the house mom and not treated badly, but still stuck in that nightmare. Since then, Lucien has walked on eggshells about her doing anything around the house, but she wanted to cook tonight. I wasn’t the one to complain about someone else cooking.

The doorbell rang as Lis walked out of her room in a cute sundress we picked up last week. The yellow flowy dress went well with her deep mahogany colored skin. Her naked, spotless face glowed in the sunlight as her lip gloss illuminated her dimples. She smiled at the similar dress Aaliyah wore as she stepped into the living room.

My beautiful sister smiled, but her eyes told a different story. Her heart was pure, and she couldn’t catch a break with men. We piled into my Audi and headed to the big city to swipe the color off Lucien's card. Four hours later, exhaustion set in, and we were ready to head home.

Stopping by the local grocery store in Blackwater, we decided on a menu for tonight, then headed in to get what we needed. As Aaliyah and I talked, she told me about her disappointment with the latest man in her life. My friend Malcolm found her and reached out to ask her on a date.

He realized she was the real deal and couldn't handle it. The vibe between them was cool, but it ended too quickly. He had her in her feelings since this was another failed attempt at dating. "Girl, I think I'm just going to be single forever."

"No. You not. You just have to be patient. It will happen when you least expect," I said, looking at her as we walked through the produce section to grab some garlic bulbs. Not paying attention to where we were going, I pushed my basket right into a man getting some fruit.

"I'm so sorry. I wasn't paying attention, running my mouth with my sister. Are you ok?"

At the impact, his head yanked back as he reached down, grabbing his leg. "I'm ok. Must have been some good gossip," he said with a chuckle as he looked between Aaliyah and me.

"No gossip. Just regular girl talk," she chimed in laughing.

"Oh! So you were talking about men. I get it." Reaching out his hand to Aaliyah, then me, he introduced himself. "I'm Adonis. Nice to meet you both." His eyes lingered a little more on Aaliyah as he spoke.

"Did you say, Adonis? As in Dr. Adonis Rane?"

"That is me. In the flesh. You look familiar, how do we know each other?" said he asked skeptically.

"We have a mutual associate. Malcolm Shore told me you were moving here soon. Said we should link based on your studies, I may be of assistance to you." I didn't want to go too in detail with listening ears around. He may be undercover for an assignment. As we spoke, I noticed his attention was on Aaliyah more than our conversation. She wasn't even paying attention to the sexy man trying to catch her eye.

"Well, it was nice to meet you, Aaliyah. Maybe we will see each other again, soon." He said, getting her attention, looking deep into her eyes. Turning to me, he said, "Definitely give me a call. I would love some help with some of my case studies at the university."

As we turned and walked off, I whisper-shouted, "Girl, he was fine!" We both laughed as she shook her head yes.

"Girl, I could climb that man like a tree," Aaliyah said as we went to look for Lisette wondering around the store.

Lisette

Being free to just be has been an adjustment for me. My twin struggled with letting me out of his sight, but at thirty-four years old, I had a lot of making up to do. I had never experienced intimate love from a man, and I think it was time to jump into the dating pool.

Before I decided to do any of that, I needed to find a hobby or a job, something to keep me occupied. I loved to cook, and Lu was finally allowing me to get in his kitchen. After convincing him that I wasn't a guest, he told me I could cook our childhood favorite meal—blackened redfish Pontchartrain with dirty rice.

Being taken out of the working girl group that was abducted, I was forced to be the house mom to all the newcomers. I knew how to cook and clean already because Má didn't play that with us. We helped in the kitchen at an early age, and cleaning was a daily ritual. Má didn't keep a dirty house.

Walking to the seafood section, I hoped they had exactly what I needed in the fresh section. A little girl stood crying, calling for her daddy; she looked no older than four years old. She was the cutest thing with her messy pigtails. "Hey, little one! Are you lost?"

She looked up into my eyes with a sheepishly terrified look on her tear-stained face. Kneeling down to her height, I held my hand out and assured her I would help her find her parents. I wiped her face with my hand before I stood up to help her look. "What's your mommy's name?"

In her little voice, she said, "I don't have a mommy anymore. She is in heaven." My heart broke at her words. A child shouldn't have to experience that at such a young age. "You seem nice. Would you like to be my mommy?"

Tears welled up in my eyes at her words. I needed to get it together before I answered.

Kneeling down, I was lost for words, but mustering all the strength I could, I said, "You are such a sweetheart. Your new mommy would be lucky to have you. Let's find your daddy, babygirl." I stood up to walk her to the front of the store when I came face to face with a hard chest and a scruffy, hard jawline.

He stood there looking deep into my eyes with a seriousness that had me fidgety under his scrutiny. His eyes were amber colored, kind of like Keisha's sister, with a golden glint. Weird. I didn't realize how common that eye color was. I needed to get out more.

"Thank you for being a Good Samaritan. I have been looking all over this place for her. Sometimes she wanders off," he said as he reached down to grab her hand. His hand brushed mine as we exchanged the little girl's hand. The deep timber of his voice and the brief brush against my skin caused a tingle to run through my body. I had never felt that sensation before. Especially not with a man. Most of my feelings were negative when it came to being in contact with men.

"Of course! I couldn't just let her cry. She is such a sweetie."

"I asked her to be my new mommy," she blurted out. We both stood shocked at her words.

"Well, baby. Uh." He was visibly uncomfortable at her words, and this big, strong man looked defeated.

In an effort to help, I cut in and said, "You know I am looking for a new gig. If you need any help with her, I would be happy to help. In my...uh other job, I took care of the new incoming women." I didn't want to tell him too much.

"Oh wow! That would be perfect. Here, take my card. Give me a call later, and we can work out the particulars," he said then hurried off. It was kind of odd, but excitement coursed through my body. I might have a new job soon.

The awkward smiling to myself was cut short when Keisha and Aaliyah popped up on me. We headed home so I could get started on the cooking. They didn't say anything immediately after, but kept hinting around, trying to get me to talk about what happened.

After we ate, Keisha and Lucien decided we all needed a movie night. Sitting on the love seat, enjoying my family, I was happy. Truly happy with where things were headed.

Thank You!

I'm so grateful for you. Thank you for spending time in my world.

What's Next?

Keep an eye out for: **Bound Whispers**

- Available for Pre-Order on Amazon.
- Signed Copies of all books are available on my website.

Let's Stay Connected

Want more secrets, bonus scenes, and behind-the-scenes magic?

Join my reader list to:

- Get exclusive content (only for subscribers)
- Access future giveaways, book updates, and early cover

reveals

- Receive a free bonus scene or epilogue not found in the book

Join the Midnight Circle—> authorstevieo.com

Loved the story? Help me grow!

If you enjoyed the book, a quick review goes a long way in helping other readers find it.Leave a review on:

- **Amazon**
- **Goodreads**

Every word you share supports an indie author chasing a dream in the dark.

With gratitude,

Stevie O. *Writer of midnight tales & dangerous hearts* |TikTok:@stevieoauthor | Instagram: AuthorStevie_O | FaceBook: Author Stevie O.

* * *

Acknowledgements

I would like to express my heartfelt thanks to everyone who helped me on this journey.

First, to my editor, Tori Moore with All That & Moore Services, for her expert editing and thoughtful feedback on this story. Her attention to detail truly helped shape this manuscript into what it is today.

Also, I appreciate Author Nastee for her guidance and encouragement during the early development of this project.

www.ingramcontent.com/pod-product-compliance
Lightning Source LLC
La Vergne TN
LVHW010655110826
845149LV00014B/3095

9798993878539